"You are ⸻
lady, Bel⸻

Feeling the col⸻
pressed her fin⸻ ⸻, you're
embarrassing m⸻

Before she could pull them back, his lips
molded themselves around her fingertips,
imprisoning them in a kiss that was more
sensual than anything she had
ever experienced.

She felt a stirring of response deep within
her. "Oh, Rex, why do you keep doing this
to me?"

"Because you keep doing it to me" was his
labored response. He signaled for their bill.
"Let's get out of here."

She felt a shiver of desire ripple through her.
Every instinct told her she should head back
to the villa before . . .

Before what? The look in Rex's eyes
promised the world, and tonight she knew
she wanted it. She wasn't running away, not
this time.

Valerie Parv had a busy and successful career as a journalist and advertising copywriter before she began writing for Harlequin in 1982. She is an enthusiastic member of several Australian writers' organizations. Her many interests include her husband, her cat and the Australian environment. Her love of the land is a distinguishing feature in many of her books for Harlequin. She has recently written a colorful study in a nonfiction book titled *The Changing Face of Australia*. Her home is in New South Wales.

Books by Valerie Parv

HARLEQUIN ROMANCE
2589—THE TALL DARK STRANGER
2628—REMEMBER ME, MY LOVE
2644—THE DREAMING DUNES
2693—MAN AND WIFE
2765—ASK ME NO QUESTIONS
2778—RETURN TO FARAWAY
2788—HEARTBREAK PLAINS
2797—BOSS OF YARRAKINA
2860—THE LOVE ARTIST
2896—MAN SHY

Don't miss any of our special offers. Write to us at the following address for information on our newest releases.

Harlequin Reader Service
901 Fuhrmann Blvd., P.O. Box 1397, Buffalo, NY 14240
Canadian address: P.O. Box 603,
Fort Erie, Ont. L2A 5X3

Sapphire Nights

Valerie Parv

Harlequin Books

TORONTO • NEW YORK • LONDON
AMSTERDAM • PARIS • SYDNEY • HAMBURG
STOCKHOLM • ATHENS • TOKYO • MILAN

Original hardcover edition published in 1987
by Mills & Boon Limited

ISBN 0-373-02909-8

Harlequin Romance first edition May 1988

Copyright © 1987 by Valerie Parv.
Philippine copyright 1987. Australian copyright 1987.
Cover illustration copyright © 1988 by Will Davies.
All rights reserved. Except for use in any review, the reproduction or utilization
of this work in whole or in part in any form by any electronic, mechanical
or other means, now known or hereafter invented, including xerography,
photocopying and recording, or in any information storage or retrieval system,
is forbidden without the permission of the publisher, Harlequin Enterprises
Limited, 225 Duncan Mill Road, Don Mills, Ontario, Canada M3B 3K9. All the
characters in this book have no existence outside the imagination of the
author and have no relation whatsoever to anyone bearing the same name
or names. They are not even distantly inspired by any individual known
or unknown to the author, and all incidents are pure invention.

The Harlequin trademarks, consisting of the words HARLEQUIN ROMANCE
and the portrayal of a Harlequin, are trademarks of Harlequin Enterprises
Limited; the portrayal of a Harlequin is registered in the United States Patent
and Trademark Office and in the Canada Trade Marks Office.

Printed in U.S.A.

CHAPTER ONE

THE twin moons of Iona hung low over the blue-purple landscape, flooding the craggy line of hills with violet light.

From the protection of her observation station, Sapphire looked out over the landscape with pleasure. As the first Earther born in the colony, she felt totally at home here, for she knew no other.

A figure darkened the landscape and she looked up, her responses as automatic as the environmental controls on the panel in front of her. Rafe Telstar was coming. She knew it as surely as she knew how to breathe.

Intently, she watched his tall figure striding over the rugged ground towards her station.

He was coming to relieve her, her watch being over for the shift. How she wished they could do more than nod in passing! Sharing the next watch with him would be far preferable. In the off-duty hours they had shared at the colony, she had learned to cherish his adventurous spirit which made him a part of this place even though he did not share her fortune in being born here.

But there was only room in the bubble for one. Reluctantly, she keyed the release which turned her protective suit over to auto control, releasing her from her symbiosis with the bubble. The lifeline sprang away from her suit and snaked back into its socket on the panel. She was free to return to the colony, as soon as Rafe took over the station.

He had almost reached the bubble when the Viand leapt from behind a pile of rocks and bowled him to the ground. Sapphire saw his weapon spin out of his hand.

'Rafe!' she screamed, the sound echoing inside her helmet. She had to do something before the Viand's claws shredded Rafe's body suit, exposing him to the hostile Ionic atmosphere. Inspiration struck and she scooped up the laser torch which she would have used to light her way back to the colony, then vaulted out of the bubble.

As she circled the Viand, Rafe stirred and regained his feet. He saw her and motioned her away, but she held her ground and hefted the torch, gesturing that he was to catch it. He did so, deftly.

As the Viand lunged for him, Rafe threw the switch on the torch, sending its pure laser light into the creature's pale, small eyes.

As a creature of darkness, it shunned strong light and there was no stronger than the laser torch. The Viand roared and shielded its eyes with its claws, then stumbled away behind the rock piles.

At once, Rafe strode to her side and caught her in an embrace as close as their protective suits would allow. She could see he was trying to be angry with her for risking her own life, but behind his face shield, his fierce expression could not hide the tenderness he felt for her.

'That's more like it!' Belle Fraser sighed with satisfaction as she pulled the sheet of paper out of her typewriter. In her first draft of *Sapphire Nights*, Sapphire had been the one to wield the laser, scaring off the creature. It worked better when Rafe and Sapphire were in partnership. Now if she could only get them together romantically...

She jumped up and walked to the expanse of glass which overlooked the Great Barrier Reef. The lushness of the tropical Queensland vegetation fringing golden sand taunted her with its invitation to surf and sun.

With all this at her feet, why had she agreed to turn an embryo screenplay into a science-fiction novel, and in just two months?

She turned away from the breathtaking view and grimaced at the typewriter. She knew perfectly well why she had agreed—to have something of her own she was good at; instead of just being Mitchell Fraser's daughter, following in his acting footsteps and, it was implied if not stated, getting parts because of her name.

Well, she had written the book, or at least most of the first draft. There was a lot of editing and retyping to do before she could show it to Andy Wakefield, the literary agent who had suggested she turn her play into a book. He had read her notes, written between her scenes in a TV film, and had asked her to try her hand at the book. If she hadn't seen the flicker of doubt on her father's face when she had mentioned it, she doubted whether she would have agreed.

Remembering her father's reaction reinforced her determination to succeed with the book. All she needed now was a satisfying conclusion, and her characters were almost there.

With a sigh, she returned to the keyboard. Under her flying fingers, Rafe began to fall in love with Sapphire, the outcome as inevitable as a beautiful sunrise on Mana Island.

Suddenly Belle's fingers froze on the keys as she became aware of a surging warmth deep inside her. A shudder shook her from head to toe and she pressed her elbows close into her sides. Good grief, she had worked herself into a frenzy just writing the last scene! She chuckled ruefully. It must be good stuff if it could arouse its author to such an extent. On the other hand, it had been a long time since she and Ted split up. Maybe she was just sex-starved.

'Hello! Anybody home? Mr Fraser... are you there?'

'In the study, come on through,' she called, marvelling that the island was one of the few places in the world where one could issue such an invitation without fear.

She looked up curiously as a young man in Mana Island T-shirt and shorts came in, lugging a heavy carton.

'They must be the groceries I ordered,' she said, remembering her phone call to the colony's store this morning.

The young man looked puzzled. 'I was told the order was for Mr Fraser. Are you his housekeeper?'

She shook her head. 'No, I'm Mr Fraser's daughter. The account is in his name. He didn't know I was coming, so he didn't let the store know, as he normally would. The housekeeper went back to the mainland a month ago and we haven't re-placed her yet, hence the confusion.'

'I see. Then it's all right if I leave this stuff? I suppose it'll be OK if you sign for it.'

'Of course,' she laughed. 'Doreen Webster knows me well, though I haven't been to the island for ages. She'll vouch for me.'

The man relaxed when she mentioned the owner of the general store. Doreen had known Belle since she was a child, holidaying here with her famous parents, so there would be no problems with the account. It was only Belle's unplanned arrival which had complicated things. She signed the bill the young man handed to her, then dug into her pocket for some change, but he shook his head.

'No need for that, Miss Fraser. Thanks all the same.'

She'd spent too much time outside Australia, in countries where tipping was as much of a reflex as breathing, she decided, smiling to herself after the man left.

She wasn't surprised that he had expected her to be the housekeeper. Andrea had often acted as caretaker while the villa was unoccupied. It had come as a surprise to everyone when she had announced she was moving back to the mainland to live with her sister. They hadn't replaced her yet because the Frasers came here so seldom nowadays. When Belle was a little girl, they had spent every available vacation here, but that was before the fateful day eight years ago, when Cornelia Fraser's car skidded on a wet road and plunged over a cliff, killing her instantly. Belle and her father had been devastated by the accident, but the spotlight had fallen inevitably on Mitchell, the filmgoer's darling, heroic even in his hour of tragedy. At times, Belle wondered if anybody remembered that she had also lost a mother.

Belle shook her head sadly. It must be the island which was making her think of Mum so vividly. It was a tragedy and a waste, but it did no good to brood on what couldn't be changed.

Instead, she carried the groceries to the kitchen and began to put them away. The task completed, she made herself a tuna salad and iced coffee for lunch, and took them out on to the terrace so she could work on her suntan while she ate.

On the table was the letter from her father which had been forwarded here by the friend renting her house on the mainland. She'd scanned it when it arrived yesterday, promising herself a leisurely read as soon as she finished her last chapter.

She hadn't quite finished, her conscience reminded her. What the heck! She needed the break! Nibbling a crunchy stalk of celery, she opened the letter.

'My dear daughter,' Mitch began, 'I was delighted to hear that you are tackling the novel after all, and of course I wish you well with it.'

'But you expect me to fall flat on my face,' interposed Belle, her tone not so much bitter as resigned.

'I enjoyed the chance to work with you on *Leading Lady* and feel the father-daughter combination will generate excellent publicity.'

'Now I know why you agreed to a cameo role,' Belle observed. She had been suspicious when her father had settled for a straight million-dollar fee without asking for a share of the profits.

'Since I arrived in London,' her father's letter continued, 'the weather has been appalling, but I am enjoying working with so many old friends again. Frankly, Shakespeare isn't my scene, but the modern version we are filming gives me quite a bit of latitude and, thank God, they haven't stuck to the original script.'

Belle laughed aloud at this. 'Trust you to want to edit Shakespeare, Dad,' she murmured.

With his usual lightning-fast change of subject, Mitch went on, 'You have probably heard the gossip about Rex and his palimony suit. The last I heard, he and Laine Grosvenor had settled out of court for two million, but that could be media hype.

Knowing Rex, he wouldn't part with so much without a fight. How she persuaded him to let her move in with him, I'll never know. It was industry gossip that it was a set-up, but Rex never listens to anyone, and now he has quite literally paid the price. I understand he is devastated and has taken off to some grass shack in the Pacific to lick his wounds.'

There were pages more of the same, mostly film industry gossip, but Belle set the letter aside and picked up a quarter of tomato, biting into it and licking her chin clean of the succulent juice.

So Rex Marron had got his come-uppance at last, had he? She remembered him well, although she doubted whether he would remember her.

When last they had met, she had been a gangly teenager with braces on her teeth and glasses she hadn't yet traded in for contact lenses. Rex had been a protégé of her father.

Although she was inured to the sight of famous people visiting her house, Rex Marron was a special case. Every time she'd seen him on screen, he had managed to make her young heart flutter. It was a source of real rancour with her that he had never paid her the slightest attention when he had come to visit her parents.

That time, he had been forced to speak to her since she was the only one at home. He had come, he'd said, to pay his respects to Mitch after the loss of his wife.

'My father isn't here just now,' she had said haughtily, aggrieved that his condolences didn't appear to extend to her as well. Didn't he think she could feel pain or loss at her age?

That her pride might be suffering because he didn't fawn over her like many of her father's famous friends, she didn't stop to consider. She only knew that Rex Marron was one of the most heartless and pompous people she had ever met.

He had insisted on waiting for her father to return, and had proceeded to act as if she didn't exist, although she had hovered in the background while he'd waited.

His relief had been ill-masked when her father returned. She remembered how the two men had talked together as if she hadn't even been there.

In the years since then, she had seen him several times at awards dinners and industry functions when she had been her father's escort. But she had carefully avoided any contact. Rex Marron had snubbed her once, when she was feeling terribly vulnerable. He wouldn't get the chance to do it again.

That he was one of the best-looking actors of the modern generation, she tried to ignore. On-screen, he exuded charm—voltage, as it was called nowadays. In his case, high voltage was even more appropriate.

Off-screen, he lived a life reminiscent of the screen actors of the early days of Hollywood, wining and dining, and no doubt bedding, the most beautiful of his leading ladies.

How he did all that and still retained his nickname of Mister Nice Guy, Belle couldn't imagine.

No doubt a hard-working publicity manager made sure Rex's exploits didn't get into the papers. But even the most blinkered reader had to know that he'd been living with Laine Grosvenor, an English actress who was now working with Rex in most of his films.

Now he was out of pocket by two million dollars and presumably one live-in lover as well, Belle thought gleefully. Serve him right! She knew it was childish to carry a grudge all these years, but she couldn't help feeling pleased that someone was finally treating him as unfeelingly as he treated other people.

Finishing her lunch, she picked up the plate and her father's letter and returned to the kitchen where she cleaned up and put everything away. The letter she tucked into a handy drawer.

The villa showed all the signs of a house which had been closed up for ages. There was a thin film of dust over most surfaces. Since she had come here intending to work on her manuscript, she had avoided being sidetracked by the backlog of chores, but now she decided to tackle some of the more pressing ones. She could finish the final chapter in the morning and start editing in the afternoon.

Tying a scarf over her honey-gold hair, she wrapped one of Andrea's old aprons around her shorts and halter top, and set to with a will.

Two hours later, the cane furniture gleamed and the parquet floor was polished to a glorious patina. A bowl of fuchsia-coloured hibiscus was reflected off the glass-topped coffee table, and the air was fragrant with the scents of tropical flowers.

She looked around with satisfaction, carefully avoiding the typewriter with its half-finished page still in the machine. She had earned some time off.

A scrabbling noise at the door startled her out of her reverie. Who could it be? She hadn't ordered anything other than the groceries, and they were already here.

'Well—hello there!'

For a moment, she was rooted to the spot in astonishment, wondering if she had conjured the man up out of her father's letter. She could hardly believe she was looking at Rex Marron himself.

Evidently, the recognition wasn't mutual. 'You must be Mitch Fraser's housekeeper, Andrea,' he said, taking in her apron-covered clothes and the scarf around her hair.

'Er...you've caught me by surprise, Mr Marron,' she said stupidly.

He didn't seem surprised at her recognition, but he was probably used to that. 'I understand, Andrea. Mr Fraser told me I could use his villa for a few weeks' rest. It was just what I needed to get me away from the media for a while.'

So he was licking his wounds in a grass shack in the Pacific, was he? Belle thought grimly. Knowing Mitch, he had probably issued the invitation as a throwaway line. He couldn't have expected Rex to take him up on it or he would have warned the man that the villa wasn't staffed at the moment. Now that Rex was here, what was she to do?

She opened her mouth to explain who she was, but before she could speak Rex said airily, 'My bags are on the terrace, honey. You can unpack them for me later. Right now, what I really need is a cold drink.'

Belle felt as though he had poured the cold drink over her. He hadn't changed a bit! He was still arrogant and demanding, still looking straight through people he considered unimportant. Well, she would show him! This time she wasn't sixteen years old, and he had just handed her a sweet means of getting her revenge while teaching him a lesson in how to treat people. 'Of course I'll get your drink, Mr Marron. I'm forgetting myself, aren't I? You just make yourself comfortable here.'

He patted her arm indulgently. 'It's OK, Andrea. I'm used to people being thrown off balance by my presence.'

Well, bully for him! she thought furiously, shrugging off his touch. He was so used to people gazing at him in mute adoration that he hadn't noticed the lack of any such emotion in her gaze. In fact, he didn't seem to remember her at all and was treating her with the same indifference she recalled only too well.

'I'll get your drink,' she said shortly, turning away. She blessed her training at the Drama Institute. This was role-playing with a vengeance. The only question was: how long could she keep up her act before she gave him a piece of her mind?

Without asking, she served him a tall gin and tonic, garnished with lemon and mint leaves. When she offered him the tray containing the glass, he looked with interest at the wide expanse of cleavage revealed over the gaping top of the apron. Clearing his throat, he took a sip of the drink before commenting, 'I expected someone older, Andrea. How long have you been with Mr Fraser?'

'Oh, years and years,' she said airily, wondering how he would react if she told the truth: that she had been with Mitchell Fraser all her life! 'I...er...came to him quite young,' she added wickedly.

'I see. How old are you?'

'Twenty-four,' she said without thinking. But she could hardly lie, since she barely looked her age anyway. There was no way she could convince him she was much older, at least not without stage make-up.

'And you live with your family on the island?' he hazarded.

It was too good to resist. 'No, I live here. Mr Fraser gives me the freedom of the villa. I often use the pool in the early morning or the evening after I finish work.'

He looked uncomfortable. 'Then I can hardly deny you the same privileges, can I? But I wonder...I mean...it doesn't look too good, for your sake, I mean.'

This was so rich that she almost choked with suppressed laughter. The man whose live-in lover had just taken him to the cleaners to the tune of two million dollars was worried about how it would *look* if he shared the villa with a young woman?

'I'm sure it will be all right,' she said gravely. Inwardly she shook with laughter. 'On Mana Island people keep very much to themselves. Most of the homes in the Colony are owned by prominent people who value their privacy and respect other people's.' It was the main reason why people like Mitchell Fraser liked coming here so much.

Sidling up to him, she flicked an imaginary speck of dust off his safari-suit jacket. 'In any case, I'm sure Mr Fraser would want you to enjoy *all* the amenities of his villa, Mr Marron.'

She didn't know what imp of mischief made her add this last. She hadn't intended to take her charade anywhere near that far, but Rex Marron's look of discomfort only encouraged her.

He took a long pull on his drink. 'I...er...didn't realise the villa was...er...staffed full-time.'

'Oh yes, all day and...' she added a purr to her voice, 'all night as well.'

'Look, I don't think I'll be staying long after all, Miss...er...Andrea. Just the one night, probably.

I didn't make any definite arrangements with Mr Fraser, so he won't mind a change of plans.'

So she was right—Mitch's invitation had been a casual impulse. She almost glowed with triumph. Not only was she getting even with Rex Marron for ignoring her all those years ago, she would soon have the villa to herself again. 'Whatever you say, Mr Marron,' she agreed, managing to sound disappointed. 'Shall I unpack for you now?'

'No, don't!' he almost exploded, then said more calmly, 'Please don't trouble yourself. I'll just get my overnight things and the rest can stay in the hallway until I leave in the morning.'

He went outside, presumably to get his things, and Belle crammed the back of her hand against her mouth, almost choking with suppressed laughter. Pretending she was a live-in maid at Rex's beck and call had been an inspiration! Now all she had to do was keep up her act until he went away again, and she could go on with her working holiday.

By the time he returned, carrying a leather overnight case embossed with his initials, she was busily plumping up the sofa cushions. She straightened when he came in. 'I'll show you to your room.'

As she had intended, he followed her, unable to avoid noticing that underneath her apron was no maid's uniform. The figure-hugging shorts barely skimmed the tops of her sleek, tanned thighs, and the halter top exposed most of her back. She heard his breathing quicken as he followed her.

She looked back at him over her shoulder, smiling as she saw his gaze fly from her taut bottom to her face. 'I'll put you in the Hibiscus room. It has the most spectacular view.'

'Whatever you say,' he repeated.

The room was actually a suite with its own bathroom and tiled terrace overlooking the ocean. He barely glanced at it when she asked it if was to his liking, and all but pushed her out of the door, saying he would take care of himself now.

In the hallway, she leaned against the wall and shook from head to toe with mirth. What would the newspapers say if they could see the screen idol, Rex Marron, whose latest indiscretion had just cost him a fortune, reduced to a quivering wreck because a 'maid' had propositioned him?

What was he so worried about? she wondered after a few minutes. Hollywood was full of dollybirds like 'Andrea'. A man with Rex's reputation shouldn't react like a gauche teenager, surely? Maybe he was still recovering from the shock of his settlement with Laine Grosvenor.

Or maybe his reputation was as much a Hollywood invention as her Andrea-character.

Somehow, she hoped it was the former rather than the latter. If he had been set up by Laine Grosvenor, then it meant his Mister Nice Guy reputation was the real one, and Belle was taking advantage of his vulnerability. Yet he hadn't cared about her vulnerability when she was a teenager.

Her good humour had evaporated with her dilemma. Oh well, he had said he was leaving in the morning so, whatever the true situation, it would be resolved then.

All the same, she felt uncomfortable at the prospect of keeping up her charade for even a short time.

Deciding to keep out of his way as much as possible, she headed for the kitchen. Cooking him a meal would help ease her conscience, she decided.

Although she had grown up surrounded by staff, Belle had chosen to learn how to fend for herself when she left school, in case the time ever came when she had no choice. Learning to cook and keep house had been more enjoyable than she had expected, and now she actually preferred looking after herself.

She bustled around the kitchen with practised ease. Soon, she had assembled a crisp avocado salad and fillets of coral trout were sizzling in butter.

By the time Rex emerged, she had set a place for him in the dining-room, having decided she would eat in the kitchen. She didn't think he would like eating with the hired help, and she wasn't sure she could keep up her Andrea act all through dinner.

He came into the kitchen looking heart-stoppingly good-looking in cream slacks and a lemon shirt, his dark hair glistening from the shower. 'Won't you eat with me?' he asked when he saw the arrangements.

She looked away, disconcerted by the unhappiness she glimpsed in the sea-green eyes. 'I'd really rather not.'

'A short time ago, you were offering me much more than company for dinner,' he reminded her.

Touché! 'Very well, I'll join you,' she agreed reluctantly. 'Dinner will be on the table in a few minutes.'

She needed the time to compose herself for the ordeal ahead. Now that he was feeling more relaxed, the famous Marron charm was all too evident. She didn't want to spoil her scheme for getting even with him by starting to like him too much.

It would be easy enough, she found out during dinner. They could well have been friends, rather than guest and 'maid'', from the warm and courteous way he treated her during the meal. He had recovered from his surprise at finding her here and seemed determined to win her over.

Her heart leapt to her mouth when, during dessert, he said, 'Haven't we met somewhere before?'

She shook her head. 'I would certainly remember you, Mr Marron.'

'Call me Rex, please.' He leaned forward earnestly. 'It's a pleasure to meet someone . . . ordinary. I mean, outside the film world.' When her eyes glittered with annoyance, he added, 'I know I'm putting this badly, but recently I've begun to wonder if there are any real people still out there. Everyone I've met lately seems to be wearing some sort of mask.'

She squirmed uneasily. What would he think of her mask? Not that he would find out that she was anything other than Mitchell Fraser's housekeeper. Suddenly, she was glad that he wouldn't. He seemed so grateful to meet someone who didn't want anything from him, that she hated to disillusion him.

What had happened to her desire to teach him a lesson? she wondered, scooping a melon ball into her mouth. An hour ago, she had been delighted at the prospect. Now she hoped he wouldn't find out how she had duped him. To her astonishment, she found she cared what he thought of her!

That would have to stop, she thought crossly. Next, she would be sorry he was leaving tomorrow.

'I'm surprised that Mitchell leaves you alone here so much,' Rex observed, breaking into her thoughts.

'He used to come here most weekends,' she said truthfully. 'But he's been so busy these last couple of years that he's hardly been in Australia at all.'

'Like me,' Rex agreed. 'After spending the last five years in Hollywood, I've almost started thinking of myself as an American. But there are times when I miss the wide open spaces, the Aussie humour...even the dust and the flies.'

'And the girls?'

He shook his head. 'No way! I've had it with girls, wherever they come from. They're only out for what they can get, I've decided.'

She pouted prettily. 'Thanks a lot!'

'Present company excepted, I suppose. Although you did go to some trouble to make me think you were Mitch's live-in lover, you know.'

'You sound as if you don't believe me.'

'I did at first. After talking to you, I'm convinced you're much too ingenuous to satisfy a man like Mitch Fraser.'

'So what do you think I am?' she asked, curious in spite of herself.

He thought for a moment. 'I don't know yet. I don't doubt that you work for Mitch—that was obvious when I walked in here. Maybe you're some sort of protégée of his, like I was at your age. Are you an actress?'

She had already told him so many lies, she didn't want to add another to the list. 'Yes, I am,' she confirmed.

'Have I seen you in anything?'

'I doubt it. I've only done supporting roles in television up to now, and some stage work here and in America. I'm still deciding whether I prefer to act or write.'

His eyebrow arched upwards. 'So you're a writer, as well?'

'That's just it, I don't know yet. I came here to be by myself while I worked it out.'

As the admission slipped out, she felt the colour creeping up her neck and face. Damn! Now she had blown her cover story of being Mitchell Fraser's long-time housekeeper.

Rex studied her curiously. 'I see.' Gently but firmly, he took the spoon from her fingers and set it down, then tilted her face towards him. 'You've already said more than you meant to. So how about telling me the rest, starting with who you really are?'

CHAPTER TWO

As he saw her face fall, Rex regretted forcing the issue so soon. Now he'd frightened her off with his confounded suspicions. She was probably just an acting hopeful Mitch had installed here, planning to make her his mistress eventually.

Rex had known from the moment they had met that she wasn't the woman-of-the-world she pretended to be. Why had she wanted him to think she was? Self-protection, he decided, answering his own question.

He would have to reassure her that she had nothing to fear from him. He meant what he said. He was off women, totally and permanently. When he needed a woman, it would be strictly a one-night stand, at her place for preference, and definitely no strings.

He wasn't interested in the odd mixture of gamine and sophisticate which 'Andrea' seemed to be. But that didn't mean he wasn't intrigued by her. Far from it. He was as intrigued as hell.

He cleared his throat. 'I'm sorry, Andrea or whoever you are, I withdraw the question. What's between you and Mitch Fraser is none of my business. I'm sorry I quizzed you about it.'

Her relief was pathetically obvious. 'Thanks, Rex. But I feel you have a right to know the truth about me.'

He was touched by her change of attitude. The veneer had dropped away almost completely, leaving her younger-looking. The effect was more in keeping with her translucent skin and sparkling hazel eyes. Right now, she looked about nineteen.

No, she didn't. My God, now he had it! He pulled a pair of sunglasses out of his shirt pocket and spun them across the table to her. 'Put these on.'

She stared at him, uncomprehending. 'Sunglasses? I don't...'

He picked them up and rested them on the bridge of her nose. Then he stared at the result. Fill out the cheekbones a little and put braces on the teeth... 'You're the Fraser kid,' he stated.

Her anger boiled over and she snatched the glasses from her nose and stood up. 'My name is Belle Fraser and I'm no kid.'

What a beguiling picture she made when she was provoked, he thought. Right now, the irises of her eyes were shot with gold flecks and there were red stains across each high cheekbone. Quite a picture! He had to remind himself that she had just admitted to leading him down the proverbial garden path. Reaching for her hand, he pulled her none too gently back into her seat. 'Sit down, Belle Fraser, and tell me what this is all about.'

She sat, tension in every line of her elegantly proportioned body. 'You're not mad at me for deceiving you?'

He shook his head. 'Sad maybe, but not angry.' He'd had enough practice at being let down by females recently. Why should he expect any different treatment, even from one as enticing and vulnerable as Belle?

Because the vulnerability was only skin-deep, he reminded himself. Her appearance was as much a pose as Laine's had been, and it would prove just as costly if he let it get to him. 'You must have had a reason for this charade,' he offered.

'It seems silly now, although it didn't when you first arrived.'

He felt a prickle of impatience. 'Try me.'

Idly, he noted how her already hectic colour intensified as she wrestled with herself. 'All right, but I warn you, even I think it's foolish now.' She took a deep breath. 'We first met when I was sixteen, just after my mother was killed in a car accident.'

He frowned. 'I remember meeting you somewhere, and I know I visited Mitch soon after the accident. That's right, you were the skinny kid with the braces who met me at the door.'

Even as he said it, he recognised it as an extremely unflattering description and he wasn't surprised when she winced.

'Thanks for the memory! That sort of attitude is precisely why I wanted to get even with you when you turned up here this afternoon.'

'I don't understand.'

'I told you it seemed silly in retrospect. But at the time, it didn't. At sixteen, I had a mad, passionate crush on you. I remember seeing *Rebel Rider* at least five times.'

It had been his first major role. 'I didn't know you were such a fan.'

'I wasn't for long. When you called when I was alone, I thought all my Christmases had come at once. Then you treated me as if I wasn't worthy of your notice. I disliked you from that moment onwards.'

Poor kid. He must have really hurt her feelings. If only she knew how shy he had been as a young actor, especially with female fans who seemed to want to eat him alive. 'I wish I could remember what I did to upset you,' he said frankly. 'I'm sorry if I hurt you, but I can assure you it wasn't intentional. I take it you still haven't forgiven me?'

'I might have done if you hadn't waltzed in here today, giving orders as if you owned the place.'

He sighed. 'You thought I hadn't changed in those intervening eight years, right?'

'Can you blame me for getting that impression?'

'I suppose not. But I've been under so much pressure lately, what with law suits and the media, it had to spill over some time. You just happened to be handy.'

'Apology accepted,' she said evenly, although he hadn't exactly intended to apologise. Oh well, let her think what she liked if it made what he had to say next go over any better.

'Now we've sorted things out, you'll understand why I need to have this place to myself for a while.'

Her eyes widened and something responded deep inside him. She had such magnificent, compelling eyes! But right now, the invitation to drown in them was rather more literal than he would have liked.

'Are you saying what I think you're saying?' she asked warily.

'I'm saying, I have prior claim to this villa, thanks to your father's invitation.'

'Of all the nerve! We just finish establishing how generous and compassionate you've become in the last eight years, then you announce that you're throwing me out of my father's house!'

She wasn't making this easy, but he was damned if he'd give in to her. He'd had enough of giving in to female demands to last him a lifetime. 'You're putting words into my mouth,' he said with an attempt at calmness he didn't feel. 'I merely said, since I have first claim on the place...'

'There are other secluded beach houses you could go to,' she interrupted.

'But not as secure from prying eyes as this one. In your colony of the rich and famous, everyone protects everyone else's privacy. Places like this are not easy to come by in Australia.'

'Then try Antarctica,' she said, tossing her head. 'I hear it's very private down there—just you and the penguins.'

'Will you listen to reason?' he heard himself shouting. Then he raked a hand through his hair. 'Honestly, I'm too tired for this. I only flew into Sydney two days ago and I've done two talk shows and a radio interview since then, so I haven't even had time to get over my jet lag. How about we discuss this in the morning?'

'Discuss you leaving, don't you mean?'

She was impossible, a typical, spoiled, self-centred movie brat, he thought as he headed for his room. He didn't even trust himself to say good-night, far less respond to her taunt.

Why did it have to be Rex Marron who turned up here now? Belle wondered as she got ready for bed. Try as she might to ignore it, the vestiges of her teenage crush on him were still there, and her stomach muscles cramped in response to the sounds coming from the guest room nearby. If she'd known how things were going to turn out, she would have shown him to a room far away from hers, in the guest wing, even if it did mean opening up the closed rooms. It would have been easier to handle than this exquisite torture.

She heard the bathwater running and her errant imagination pictured him stripping off his shirt and stepping out of his trousers, to stand naked and magnificent in the centre of the room. Then he would plunge into the water and droplets of moisture would bead his tanned skin.

A writer's imagination was a curse sometimes, she thought irritably, shrugging off the vision. All the same, she tossed and turned for ages, hot in spite of the villa's purring air-conditioning system.

When she finally drifted into a restless sleep, she was taunted by dreams of a man in an open-necked silk shirt, pushing aside her gracefully outstretched hand. Laughing, he said, 'Frankly, m'dear, I don't give a damn!'

Which was precisely how Rex Marron felt about her, she decided when she awoke next morning and remembered the dream.

Her eyes felt gritty and her body ached from the tossing and turning, so she decided to have a swim to refresh herself before breakfast.

Although the beach was only metres away from the front of the villa, Mitch had installed a tiled pool on the beachfront for guests who were nervous of the sharks which abounded in the waters of the Reef. Set in an oasis of pampas grass and Traveller palms, the pool gave one the impression of swimming in the ocean without any of the very real dangers.

The solar-heated water was gloriously warm when she plunged in, glad that the villa's seclusion allowed her to wear her brief string bikini. Sometimes when she was alone she didn't even wear that much, but today she was all-too conscious of Rex's presence in the villa.

She had swum several lengths and was getting her breath back in the shallow end when she heard a rustling in the pampas grass at one end of the pool. 'Who is it?' she asked, sure that Rex would have identified himself.

When there was no answer, she hauled herself up on to the tiled surround. 'I said, who's there? Identify yourself or I'll call Security,' she said imperiously, hoping the intruder would be bluffed. The colony's relative seclusion had made elaborate security precautions seem unnecessary.

She gasped with shock when a man of about thirty emerged from the bushes, brushing leaves off neatly pressed trousers.

'Who are you?'

He grinned and brushed a lock of hair back from his face in a boyish gesture. 'Sorry if I gave you a fright. I'm Harry Crossinger, journalist with the *Australian Enquirer*.'

Journalist? He must have tracked Rex here. 'You do realise you're trespassing?' she asked in the same uncompromising tone. She hoped Rex wouldn't choose the next few minutes to come in search of her.

Harry Crossinger seemed unperturbed. 'How else was I to find out if Rex Marron was holed up here?'

'Rex Marron? I should be so lucky!'

He appraised her scanty bikini appreciatively. 'I'd say Rex is the lucky one. I know he's here, so don't try to deny it. I've been writing an exposé about his palimony suit with Laine Grosvenor. All I need now is a follow-up story about his future plans, then I'll leave you both alone.'

Without really knowing why, she felt an urge to shield Rex from his pursuers. 'I'm afraid you won't find him here, so you're wasting your time,' she said breezily.

Harry Crossinger looked disappointed. 'You can do better than that—Miss Fraser, isn't it? I've seen you on the movie set with your father. I know a man arrived here yesterday and came straight to this villa. Rex Marron's trail ends where this man's begins. It has to be him.'

She thought furiously. 'There is a man staying here,' she conceded. 'My boyfriend.'

'So you're the new lady in Rex Marron's life?' the journalist persisted. 'This will make a better story than I thought.'

'I keep telling you, the man staying here isn't Rex Marron.'

The man regarded her pityingly. 'Nice try, lady. Care to tell me his name?'

All the secret identities she'd read about flashed through her mind and she seized on one. 'Er...his name's Clark...er...Clark Rider.' The combination of Superman's *alter ego* and the title of Rex's first big film seemed appropriate.

'This Clark Rider, he isn't in show business, or I'd know him.'

'No, he's...er...a security man, you know, installs burglar alarms, that sort of thing? That's how we met.' This time, she blessed her writer's inventiveness!

The ready details seemed to allay Crossinger's suspicions a little. 'I'd like to meet this Mr Rider,' he said at last.

Her heart sank. 'You can't, at least not for ages. He's a bushwalking freak and he's gone off into the nature reserve.'

'This early in the morning?'

'He's a health nut as well.'

Harry Crossinger folded his arms across his chest. 'Then I'll just have to wait until he gets back.'

This was hopeless. 'I've already told you, he won't be back for ages. Besides, if you insist on staying, I'll have to call Security and have you thrown out.'

Harry laughed. 'That would make an even better story than the one I'm after, so go right ahead.'

She sighed inwardly. 'Very well. If you'll agree to go away and come back later, I'll introduce you to Clark.'

'That's more like it. Shall we say one o'clock, then?'

'Very well. One o'clock.'

'How did he get in here?' Rex asked when she told him about the incident over breakfast.

'By boat, I expect. It's the only way in other than through the main gate to the colony, and that has a security lock.'

He nodded. 'I know. I used the key your father gave me to let myself in yesterday.'

Another possibility occurred to her. 'Mrs Webster has a new delivery man at the general store. He could have been bribed to let Crossinger in when he made his deliveries.'

'None of which really matters now. The question is, what do we tell him when he comes back to meet your friend, Clark Rider?'

'We make sure Clark is ready and waiting for him,' she said, earning a curious look from Rex.

Why she should go out of her way to help him, she didn't know. Protecting their own, her father would call it, but frankly, she didn't feel any kinship with Rex. For her, it was an accident of birth which linked them together in show business. On the other hand, she and her family had received some rough treatment by the Press in their time. It would be fun to turn the tables.

Whatever her motives, once the decision was made, she threw herself into the project of creating 'Clark Rider' with enthusiasm.

Most of her stage make-up was still at home, but she used her everyday make-up to lighten Rex's dark eyebrows and tinge his temples with grey. With his hair slicked back and a pair of her father's reading glasses perched on his nose, he looked completely different.

In one of Mitch's oversized painting shirts, its sleeves doubled back, he looked thinner and bonier, and Bell tied a tie sloppily at his neck to create an impression of dishevelment.

'How do I look?' Rex asked when she stepped back.

'Like Clark Kent's country cousin,' she grimaced. 'If this ever gets out, my friends will wonder what happened to my taste.'

'Thanks a lot!'

'Don't thank me just yet. We still have to fool the inquisitive Mr Crossinger.'

By the time the journalist arrived, they were strolling through the grounds of the villa, hand in hand and giving every appearance of being absorbed in each other.

'Don't look now, our snoopy pressman is approaching,' Rex said, leaning lovingly towards her.

'I ought to get an Oscar for this,' she responded through a wide, totally fake smile.

She turned, surprising the journalist who was sneaking up on them. 'Why, Mr Crossinger! Right on time, I see.'

'All ready to meet your boyfriend.'

Rex turned and gave the journalist a wimpy smile. 'Hi, it's so exciting to meet a real reporter. I'm Clark Rider.'

His voice! Somehow he'd changed it from Australian with Hollywood overtones, to a back-of-Bourke twang. She would also swear he had a bad case of sinusitis. The reporter took his hand and winced at the bone-cracking shake Rex gave it.

'I'm ... er ... glad to meet you, too, Mr Rider. How long are you staying on the island?'

Rex gave Belle a soppy smile. 'That depends on my sheila, doesn't it, sweetness?'

Belle felt ill. She had never been called anyone's sheila in her life. She smiled back. 'You should know how I feel about you by now, Clark.' Let him make what he liked out of that!

The reporter looked disconcerted. She could tell he was weighing up whether Belle Fraser's new romance was as newsworthy as the whereabouts of Rex Marron. Had she been with a more eligible-looking suitor, the reporter might have stayed around. As it was, he seemed anxious to get away. 'I can see I followed the wrong lead, Miss Fraser. But just in case Marron is coming here, I'll stick around for a while, maybe stake out the mainland airport, too. Tell him that if you see him, won't you?'

Then he hurried away across the lawn, skirting the pool. She turned shining eyes to Rex. 'It worked! He really believed you were Clark Rider.'

To her astonishment, instead of dropping the act right away, he gave her another sloppy smile and dropped an arm around her shoulders, drawing her close to him.

She was totally unprepared when his mouth came down on hers, but her gasp of dismay was lost in the kiss. It seemed to go on for an age, until the garden began to spin around her. His lips were warm and firm against hers and her nostrils were assailed by the cool sage scent of his aftershave lotion mingled with the make-up of his disguise.

Her throat and stomach muscles contracted and her arms crept up to twine around his neck.

Dimly, she realised she was waiting for a director to call 'cut', then just as quickly realised that this was no movie set. Rex Marron was kissing her and, what was even more incredible, she was responding with equal ardour! She pulled away from him but he kept his arm around her shoulders.

'What do you think you're doing?' she hissed.

'Just putting on an act in case our friend Crossinger decided to linger in the bushes.'

So it *was* an act, and she had been foolish enough to fall for it. 'I guessed as much,' she said stiffly. 'That's why I put on such a good performance myself.'

He looked at her shrewdly. 'Some performance—if you were really acting.'

'Of course I was. You don't think I wanted you to kiss me?'

'Why not? Lots of women do.'

He was insufferable. Reminded of his arrogance, she made a determined effort to put some distance between them. This time, he didn't stop her and she guessed that Crossinger had finally gone away. She was also hurt that he lumped her in with all the other women he had kissed. Hadn't he felt anything during the passionate exchange?

It seemed he hadn't. Removing the glasses, he said, 'You'd better start packing if you want to make the helicopter flight to the mainland.'

She stiffened. 'Oh no, you don't! I didn't agree to leave, remember? As it happens, I can't. I've lent my Sydney house to a friend while her home is being renovated. Her place won't be ready for two months and I promised she could have mine until then. In any case, this is my home.'

'Your father's home,' he corrected mildly. 'Which he gave me free access to.'

'Only because he didn't know I was here first.'

'If you telephoned him and explained the situation, what do you think would say?'

She knew perfectly well what Mitch would say. He would be apologetic, but he would put 'poor Rex's' needs ahead of his daughter's, as usual. She decided to try another strategy. 'It isn't too late for me to catch up with Harry Crossinger,' she said silkily.

'You little...you wouldn't do such a thing, would you?'

She wouldn't, but he wasn't to know that. 'I won't if you agree to take the next flight back to the mainland.'

'But if Crossinger's on it, he'll know I was here all the time and he'll hound me all the way home. These investigative types just don't know when to quit.'

He looked so genuinely distressed that she was moved in spite of herself. 'Oh, all right, you can stay,' she conceded. 'But I'm not leaving, either. We'll have to work out a way to share the villa.'

As she saw his eyes brighten with anticipation, she added hastily, 'Not in the way you think I mean, either. The place is big enough so we won't even have to see each other, except for meals.'

'What a pity. I would enjoy living with you—if you meant it literally.'

'Well, I didn't,' she added crossly, already regretting that she had agreed to let him stay. She had come here for peace and quiet, not to be distracted by a man who was disturbingly good-looking and whose kiss made her knees feel weak just thinking about it. The prospect of dodging the press for her entire stay didn't appeal to her either, but the decision was made. She may as well make the best of it.

She turned on her heel. 'Let's see how we can make this work.'

Dutifully, he followed in her wake as she went from room to room, allocating them between them. She would work in her father's study, where her equipment was already set up. He could work in the second sitting-room which had been her mother's, and was now used by guests as a television room. 'You did bring some work with you?' she asked.

'I have some scripts to look over,' he agreed. 'But mainly I was planning to lie around the pool and work on my tan.'

'We'll have to share the pool, unfortunately, and the kitchen. There's another kitchen in the guest wing but the rooms have been closed up, and you would need supplies. I can order some if you'd prefer it.'

'Oh no, I'd rather share your kitchen,' he said a shade too quickly.

'Good. If you give me an idea of your timetable, I'll make sure I use the kitchen at different times from you,' she said, forestalling him. 'Are you an early bird or a night owl?'

'A night owl, like most actors, I guess.'

'I'm atypical then, because I like the morning sun, so I'll take the first sitting for meals if it's all right with you?'

'See, it will work out perfectly,' he said happily and she looked at him suspiciously.

'You're taking all this rather well. What are you up to?'

He shrugged. 'Why should I be up to anything? You've saved me from the media wolves, now I'm trying to co-operate as best I can. I'm just wondering when the white tape comes out.'

Puzzled, she stared at him. 'What white tape?'

'The stuff you use to divide all the rooms down the middle the way they do in the TV sitcoms. In all the best comedies, everything is marked out with white tape so each party knows their limitations.'

'This isn't a game, you know. I wasn't planning to share the next few weeks with anyone and, frankly, I'm not looking forward to it.'

His eyes narrowed and his gaze became intimate. She shivered in spite of herself. 'Oh, but I am . . . looking forward to it, I mean. Coming here alone wasn't my choice, but I had to get away until all the publicity died down. It was getting so I couldn't step from my house into my car without a flashbulb going off.'

She was unmoved. 'Then you should have thought of the problems before you started playing house with Laine Grosvenor.'

Whether it was said out of pique or not, she couldn't say, but she regretted the impulse as soon as she saw a cloud descend over his expression. 'Maybe we should get that white tape, after all,' he said coldly. 'We could start by putting some over that mouth of yours, at least until you have some idea what you're talking about!'

She knew perfectly well what she was talking about. Every detail of his relationship with the actress, and the subsequent expensive break-up had been reported in print and on television.

For the first time, she wondered if there was more to the story than anyone knew. 'You'll find I'm not so easy to gag,' she warned him, hurt nevertheless. 'But since we agreed to have separate visits here, I suppose we should also keep our affairs separate as well. Good morning.'

With head held high, she stalked off, keeping carefully to the rooms she had earmarked for herself. She understood his reluctance to leave the island while it was being watched by the Press, but she wasn't sure how long they could keep up this crazy existence. It was all very well to agree to keep everything separate while they shared the house, but they had already shared more than she cared for.

A kiss, for one thing.

She touched a finger to her lips, tasting his embrace yet again. He had been acting for the benefit of the journalist, she knew, but all the same, the strength of her response had shaken her. She had been kissed often enough since she was a child—kissing being the film world's equivalent of a handshake—but no exchange had stirred her senses as powerfully as Rex's kiss today.

She would have to be careful, she warned herself. He had already told her he wanted no more women in his life, so she was playing with fire if she became involved with him. Not that she planned to, of course. She had no time for self-centred men like him, either.

So why was she so stirred by the thought of being in his arms? It was almost as if she wanted a repeat of the experience, which was nonsense. She had more sense than that.

In any case, he kept his word and stayed in his designated rooms for the rest of the day. She saw him only briefly when they met in the kitchen to make coffee. The galley kitchen had cupboards ranged down both sides, with a door at each end, so they were forced to pass each other to fetch cups and fill them from the percolator.

His hip brushed her thigh as he manoeuvred past her and she tensed at the surge of feeling which jolted her. 'I'm sorry, did I bump you?' he asked in concern.

How could she tell him that the slight contact had jarred her to her core? Her body felt drawn to his, hungry for the contact as if they were two magnetised particles. Hastily, she moved away. 'What time do you want to use the kitchen for dinner?'

'Any time. I'm not much of a cook so it won't take me long to throw something together. I'll put in half the grocery costs, by the way.'

'There's no need. Everything is charged to Dad's account and, since you're here on his invitation, he wouldn't want you to pay anything.'

'All the same, I'd prefer to pay my own way.'

'As you like.'

Her store of small talk was used up, so she had no option but to return to the study and go on with her writing. It was a pleasant enough task, but every time Sapphire and Rafe made love, Belle went off into a daze in which she was the one in Rafe's arms.

The colony was ablaze with lights to celebrate the Festival of Twin Moons, the magical time when the single colonists elected to choose their mates.

For Sapphire, there was no choice—ever since the moment when they had faced the attacking Viand together at the outpost, she had known Rafe was the only mate for her.

They had chosen the toughest assignment of all, to pioneer the far-flung desert regions of the planet, but Sapphire knew there could be no hardship too great to endure, as long as Rafe was at her side.

The marriage ceremony was so beautiful, it moved Belle to tears. Then she had the greatest fun creating a desert region sufficiently challenging for characters like Rafe and Sapphire to conquer in style.

That Rafe bore a striking resemblance to Rex Marron, she hated to admit. He was every bit as masculine and all-conquering, but, she told herself, he had the redeeming quality of consideration for others—not at all like Rex.

Lost in her galactic fantasy, she was jolted back to reality by a crash from the kitchen which reverberated through the villa.

It sounded as if every saucepan in the place had been dropped at once.

Before she could rush to investigate, the crash was followed by a torrent of language which was not only colourful, but highly inventive. Many of the words were new to her and she wondered where Rex had picked them up.

'What on earth is the matter?' she demanded, bursting into the kitchen.

She stood stock-still, transfixed by the sight of the world's most eligible actor, spattered from head to toe in spaghetti sauce, with strands of pasta hanging from his earlobes like punk earrings.

He gave her a lop-sided grin. 'I'm cooking my dinner.'

CHAPTER THREE

REX lifted his fork and prodded the mound of golden pasta sprinkled with freshly chopped parsley. 'I hope this isn't the same stuff I was wearing in the kitchen.'

Belle suppressed her laughter as the vision of a spaghetti-clad Rex rose up before her. She would never forget that sight as long as she lived. 'Of course not,' she chuckled. 'I threw yours out and made a fresh batch while the marinara sauce was cooking.'

He took a mouthful. 'Mmm, this is good. Not that I couldn't have done as well, given the chance. After all, accidents can happen to anyone.'

'Anyone who can't cook. Confess, you can't.'

There was a definite twinkle in his eye as he faced her across the table. 'All right, I confess. But I was determined to give it a try, since you were so set on us having separate holidays under the same roof.'

'A lot of good it did me! I ended up cooking dinner for two, anyway.'

She should sound more annoyed about it, in case he thought he could expect the same treatment every night, she thought, but her voice came out soft and indulgent instead of reproving. The truth was, she had enjoyed preparing their meal tonight. It was pleasant to have someone to cook for. On the rare occasions when she had cooked for her father, he had either failed to comment, or had suggested she leave the domestic chores to his highly paid housekeeper.

She offered Rex the bowl of marinara sauce, reminding him that the seafood she had used was freshly caught in the waters surrounding the island. He heaped his plate and dug into it enthusiastically.

With a longing look at the glistening pasta, she reached for the salad bowl. Until she was sure she could make it as a writer, she had better keep watching her recalcitrant figure. A fat actress was usually an unemployed actress.

'How do you manage when you're at home?' she asked Rex.

'You mean cooking? Mostly I eat out. If I'm entertaining, I have caterers. Luckily, I'm not in my own kitchen long enough to cause the kind of disaster I created in yours.'

'Which explains why you can't drain spaghetti without wearing it,' she observed.

'You could come and give me cooking lessons,' he suggested unexpectedly. 'Watching you in the kitchen tonight was kind of homey.'

From which she could deduce that Laine Grosvenor wasn't much of a cook, either. Living with Laine, he would have had ample opportunity to watch her in the kitchen otherwise. 'I'm glad you enjoyed the experience,' she said a little tartly, her mood soured by this thought. 'Luckily, Doreen

Webster's store carries a good range of TV dinners for people like you.'

He looked disappointed. 'It sounds as if this is to be my first and last home-cooked meal. Pity. I like having you bail me out of trouble.'

He was referring to this morning's adventure with the journalist, she supposed. She grinned in spite of herself. 'I am making a habit of it, aren't I? It's a shame you can't return the favour for me.'

His curiosity was aroused, she could see from the way he ignored the pasta momentarily, to give her his full attention. 'Is there something I can do to help you?'

She shook her head. 'Unfortunately not. I got myself into a hole by agreeing to adapt a film script of mine into a science-fiction novel. It's harder than I thought.'

'And it isn't going well?'

'That's just it, I don't know. It's the first such project I've tackled. I've written a few screenplays, but they've never seen the light of day. I just write them and stick them in a drawer.'

He frowned. 'You of all people should know you can't do any good that way. Writing is like acting. It isn't a complete transaction until you have an audience, or in this case, a reader.'

'You're right, of course. And I do intend to send this book to a publisher. I won't have any choice as it happens, because I was commissioned to write it.' She explained about Andy Wakefield reading her screenplay and arranging a publishing contract for her to write the novel. 'So you see, I'm committed to doing it.'

Rex refilled her glass with the excellent Pinot Noir they were enjoying with the food. 'I didn't know writing talent ran in your family.'

She took a sip of her wine before answering. 'It doesn't. Which is precisely why I want to make a success of it.'

He looked baffled. 'I'm not with you.'

She hadn't intended to tell anyone her reasons for writing the book, but suddenly, she had a feeling Rex would understand, and it would be good to share her feelings with someone. 'As an actress, I'll always be Mitchell Fraser's daughter, an echo. If I'm good, it's because I've inherited his talent; if I'm terrible, it's because I haven't. At least when it comes to writing I can stand or fall by my own abilities.'

Rex's eyes were full of sympathy. 'It must be tough coming from such a famous family, especially losing your mother the way you did.'

She nodded, her eyes misting. 'It sounds dreadful to admit it, but I still get twinges of jealousy over Mum, even though she's gone. She was so talented. I can never measure up to her as an actress.'

He exhaled slowly. 'Quite a load to carry. I suppose you were expected to step right into your mother's shoes after the accident.'

'I'm afraid so. Only I didn't turn out to be very good at it, so Dad finally gave up on me.'

'Which may be a good thing if it takes some of the pressure off you and allows you to find your own way in life.'

Surprised, she glanced at him. 'I hadn't considered it like that. But I suppose you're right.' She forced a smile. 'I shouldn't really complain. Having such a successful father had advantages, too. I've never had to worry about money or security.'

He paused in the act of swabbing his plate with a piece of crusty bread. 'Yet you can cook—and keep house, as I saw for myself when I arrived.'

Reminded of how she had deceived him into thinking she was Mitchell's housekeeper, she flushed. 'Well, at least you know my domestic talents are genuine. They're part of my declaration of independence.'

He frowned. 'Does that include independence from men?'

'Definitely. The ones I've known up to now only wanted me for my name, or to prove they could dominate a well known woman.'

'Sounds like you haven't had much luck with your men.' He leaned across the table. 'But didn't I hear you were all but engaged?'

Damn the show-business grapevine! She should have known he would have heard about her relationship with Ted . . . her past relationship, she added inwardly. 'Then you heard wrong,' she said aloud and stood up, reaching for the dishes.

He stacked the plates and handed them to her. 'Don't talk about it if you'd rather not,' he said gently. 'I know what it's like to have your private life smeared all over the place, remember? But it might help to get it off your chest.'

After a slight hesitation, she sat down again, feeling again that he would understand how she felt. It was extraordinary, because she had never experienced such a feeling of empathy with anyone, least of all her father. 'You're right,' she conceded. 'It is nice to talk to someone who's been through the same mill.'

'So what happened?'

Despite her vow to keep their affairs separate, she found she wanted to talk to Rex about Ted. It had been bottled up inside her for too long. If the media found out . . . she shuddered at the thought. Seeing the reaction, Rex rested his hand on hers. The light touch sent a jolt like electricity surging through her, lending her a curious kind of strength.

She took a deep breath and plunged in. 'Ted Koenig was the costume designer on a play I was in. Seeing him every day for fittings, we started talking. That led to coffee after the show and before I knew it . . .'

'You had a full-blown affair going,' Rex guessed.

'I did, anyway. I'm still not sure about him. At first, I really thought he cared about me, not my name or my money, but me. We had wonderful times together. We had so much in common.'

Rex's hold on her hand tightened a fraction. 'Why do I get the feeling there's a "but" coming?'

'Because there is. I was so convinced that Ted was the man for me that I took him home to meet Dad. They got on well and the photo albums came out. Dad was charmed by Ted's apparent fascination with the family. What he still doesn't know is...' Her voice cracked and she looked away, trying to pull her hand from Rex's grasp.

He held her fast. 'Whatever it is, you can talk about it. It will fester and grow otherwise.'

She smiled weakly. 'Sounds like the voice of experience.'

'It is. Go on.'

She took a steadying breath, but her voice was still hoarse when she finally forced the words out. 'It turned out that Ted had a morbid fascination with my mother. That's why he was so interested in the old photos. He dressed me like her in the show and suggested a similar hairstyle. I didn't realise what he was trying to do until he...he tried to talk me into going to a seance with him to try to get in touch with her.'

She wasn't aware that Rex had moved until she felt his arms go around her shoulders. 'How terrible for you,' he said and when she opened her eyes, he looked genuinely shocked—but for her, not at the revelation. 'I remember how devastated you were over your mother's death. It can't have helped, having him drag it up again in such a bizarre way.'

When she finally absorbed the full import of this, she stared at him open-mouthed. 'I thought you didn't remember our first meeting.'

He looked uncomfortable. 'It seemed kinder not to, until you mentioned it. You weren't yourself that day, so prickly and stand-offish.'

'Me? Stand-offish? You were the one who wouldn't take any notice of me.'

'From the way you greeted me, I got the impression that you thought I was intruding on your family grief,' he said quietly.

Seen from his point of view, it did look different from the way she remembered their meeting. 'So you were being kind, leaving me alone,' she guessed. 'You make me feel so small. I thought you were rude and arrogant, and I've held that day against you all these years.'

She began slowly to clear the table. Without asking, he helped her stack the dishes and carry them to the kitchen where he leaned against a cupboard and watched as she loaded the dishwasher. 'What were you—all of sixteen?' She nodded. 'So your judgement was a little off. I made some stupid mistakes myself at that age. The point is, am I forgiven now?'

'You would have been forgiven long ago if I hadn't been so stubborn. We could have been friends all these years if I hadn't misunderstood your motives.'

'Which almost sounds as if you regret it.'

This was getting much too intense for two people who were supposed to be having a no-strings vacation together. She closed the dishwasher, programming it with fierce concentration.

When the machine began to whir and splash, she looked up again, once more composed. This time she succeeded in keeping her tone light. 'You know what teenage crushes are? I remember a girl sending Dad a letter which had "I love you, Mitchell Fraser" written on it twenty thousand times on this long streamer of paper. She'd spent days doing it and when he got it, Dad didn't know what on earth to say. Crushes are like that, matters of life and death until you get over them.'

'Just as well you're over yours then, isn't it?' he said in a curiously hard voice.

Why did he sound so disturbed by what should have relieved him? she wondered. 'Yes, it is,' she said brightly, hoping she wasn't overdoing things. 'At least now we can be friends on an adult level.'

Without responding, he led the way out of the kitchen back to the living-room where he went to the bar and poured liqueurs for them both. He had selected her favourite, Grand Marnier. She accepted it and dropped on to the couch opposite him. 'That's enough about me,' she said determinedly. 'Now it's your turn. Did you always want to be an actor?'

As if he sensed the fear behind her withdrawal, he grinned disarmingly. The smile said, 'I'm aware of your strategy but I'll go along for now.' Aloud, he said, 'Actually, I never thought of acting as a career.'

'Yet you made a career of it.'

'It was the only thing I knew how to do. My mother made very sure of that. If my Dad had lived...'

So he had his private sorrows, too. 'I didn't know your mother was in show business,' she said by way of distraction.

'She was famous in the English theatre before she married my father and came to live in Australia. He didn't think a wife should have a career, so she gave it up. But it didn't stop her hoping I would be an actor. She did everything she could to foster my interest, buying me books, sending me to classes. If Dad had allowed it, she would have taken me to auditions even as a child.'

'But your father was against it?'

Rex nodded. 'He wanted me to take over his grazing property when he retired, so I had a curiously mixed upbringing—part jackeroo, part actor. For many years, I wasn't sure myself to which world I really belonged.'

'What happened to help you decide?' she asked curiously.

His expression became pained. 'Dad was a qualified pilot and flew his own light plane. One day, he was flying Mum and me home to the country after a visit to Sydney, when the engine cut out. He made an emergency landing, but the plane jackknifed at the end of the paddock. He was killed. Mum was badly injured, but she ignored her own injuries to drag me free of the plane before it exploded. If it hadn't been for her, I would have died.'

A wave of compassion washed over her and she yearned to take Rex in her arms and offer him the same comfort he had offered her. What held her back, she wasn't sure. Perhaps it was the instinctive sureness that if she held him now, she wouldn't want to let go.

'I'm sorry, I didn't know any of this,' she breathed.

His face cleared abruptly. 'Thanks, but it's ancient history now. It made headlines at the time because Mum was still well known. After the fuss died down, she sold the country property and moved to an apartment in Sydney.'

'So you never got the chance to follow in your father's footsteps.'

Rex shrugged. 'Call it fate, but it saved me from making the choice. As soon as I was old enough, Mum enrolled me in a school which specialises in the performing arts. With Dad gone, there wasn't much for me in the country, and at least studying acting, I was doing something I knew I could do well. I threw myself into my studies, was moderately successful at it and ... the rest is history. But I didn't start to really love acting until your father took me under his wing and taught me to understand my craft.'

'And your mother?'

'She's the reason I try to work at least some of the time in Australia, otherwise I might have become an American citizen. She was never the same after the plane crash. Her lungs were damaged, and recently her health really began to deteriorate. Her nerves are affected, too. The doctors warned me that the slightest upset could push her over the edge into complete nervous collapse.'

Suddenly her own family concerns seemed minor. At least her father still had his health and strength. 'What a terrible dilemma,' she said, heartfelt.

'I was in a cold sweat about her at first, but I've come to accept the situation. All I can do is protect her from worry as much as possible.'

'Do you have brothers or sisters to share the burden?'

He shook his head. 'There's only Mother's companion, a retired English actress who worked with Mother in the old days. I don't know what we would have done without her.'

'Does your mother live with you?'

'She refused to move in with me when I asked her, preferring her own apartment with her theatrical memorabilia and her reminders of Dad.'

Was Rex's mother the reason behind Laine Grosvenor's defection? Belle couldn't help wondering. Laine didn't seem the type to want to be burdened with the problems of an ailing older woman.

'I see,' she said heavily.

As if he read her thoughts, his eyes darkened. 'What do you see?'

The sharpness in his tone startled her. 'I only meant I could see why your life has been so...er...complicated lately.'

His lip curled into a sneer. 'I know exactly what you meant. Like everybody else, you think you know the story of my life. Well, you don't. Nobody does.'

She felt her eyes prickle with tears at the unfairness of his attack. 'I only know what you've told me tonight,' she defended herself. 'And I didn't exactly have to worm the details out of you.'

Subsiding as suddenly as he had erupted, he passed a hand across his eyes. 'I'm sorry, Belle. I didn't mean to imply anything. You've been a damned good listener tonight and I'm glad I told you the things I did. But so much has been written about me lately, most of it outright lies, that I reacted automatically. Am I forgiven?'

Although she accepted his apology she couldn't help wondering about what he'd said. So some of the stories were untrue—but which ones? He could hardly deny that he had been living with Laine, so perhaps the amount he had paid her in palimony was exaggerated. Nothing to get so angry about, surely? She jumped as his hand brushed her cheek.

'You're still angry,' he said.

'No, I'm not,' she argued, then softened as his charm began to affect her. 'All right, maybe a little. You did sound like a bear with a sore head, and for no good reason.'

'Oh, I had reason,' he said ruefully, adding quickly, 'but not to sound off at you. Tell you what, will a moonlight swim help to make it up to you?'

The night was crystal clear and balmy, with the faintest sea breeze and traces of puffy clouds scudding across the star-bright sky. The perfect night for swimming. 'All right,' she said on impulse. 'I'll go and change.'

But as she stirred, his touch restrained her. 'What do you need a swimsuit for? There's nobody here but us.'

She knew that nude swimming was readily accepted in Hollywood, where Rex spent so much of his time. On a visit there, she had even gone to Gaviota Pass herself for a dare. It was also common at the show business parties she'd attended. But she still didn't feel comfortable swimming naked in front of other people, although she enjoyed it in private.

He noticed the indecision on her face. 'You're not shy, are you? When I came to your father's pool parties, you used to swan around in next to nothing without a care.'

'I was sixteen and stupid,' she retorted. 'Besides, who could be aroused by an ugly duckling like me?'

'I could argue that point, but it's more likely to scare you off than persuade you. You do what you think best. I just hope you don't mind me not wearing a suit.'

'Of course not,' she said a little too emphatically. 'But I'll wear my bikini, if you don't mind.'

His look plainly said he did mind, but he accepted her decision with good grace. 'I'll meet you at the pool.'

He was already swimming strongly up and down the pool by the time she emerged, clad in her minuscule string bikini. On reflection, it was ridiculous to put her faith in such a tiny garment, but she felt better approaching the pool with it on.

He kept swimming as she slid into the velvety water which was as warm as a bath, so she joined him in swimming laps. For a time, they kept up a steady, companionable rhythm as their lithe bodies cut twin swathes through the dark water.

At last her lungs demanded rest, and she swam sidestroke to the tiered steps let into the side of the pool, stretching out on the lowest one so she was still covered in water, but could rest her weight on the surround.

Rex swam up to her and a shiver ran down her spine as he stretched out beside her, the moonlight glinting off his tanned body. Water rippled around his hips, shielding him from her, but her imagination began to work overtime.

He was magnificent, just as firm and lean as she had imagined. There were no telltale white patches—at least none she could see—so he probably sunbathed in the nude, too. Still, a suntan was part of his stock-in-trade, as were the rippling muscles and flat stomach, she decided. His marvellous physique was frequently mentioned when his films were reviewed.

'You must spend a lot of time in a gym,' she speculated, not realising she had spoken aloud until he quirked an eyebrow at her.

'If a man made such a comment he'd be accused of treating a woman as a sex object.'

Since her remark had been fairly innocent, confusion made her answer a little sharply. 'Well, aren't you a sex object? It's what you've spent your career trying to become, after all.'

The amusement vanished from his gaze. 'That's bloody unfair, as well as being untrue. I've spent my time trying to establish myself as a serious actor. I can't help the way I look.'

'But you don't deny that you exploit your looks?'

'I use my body to create a character,' he said evenly, plainly annoyed by the discussion. 'What would you have me do—have plastic surgery to make me ugly?'

In truth she had been using the discussion as a means of putting some distance between them, mentally if not physically. She was all-too conscious of his naked presence beside her, and there was a fierce, quivering sensation deep in the pit of her stomach which threatened to engulf her if she wasn't careful. It must be the vestige of her teenage crush, because he wasn't the sort of man who attracted her nowadays, was he?

'I didn't say any such thing,' she snapped back. Discussing his body was the last thing she had intended to start doing, and now she couldn't think how to change the subject gracefully. 'You started this by accusing me of being sexist.'

He fixed her with a disturbingly direct stare. 'I didn't start anything, Belle. I think you provoked a row with me to avoid acknowledging the obvious.'

She stirred restively in the shallows. 'Which is?'

'It's not the other women filmgoers finding my body attractive which worries you. It's your own reaction. So you mock me rather than face the truth.'

He really hadn't changed since she knew him in her teens. 'Of all the conceited, big-headed...'

Whatever else she had to say was drowned out when he rolled over and pinned her to the steps with the weight of his body. His skin was slick with water and the hands she raised to ward him off skidded ineffectually down his back.

She thought he meant to kiss her, but he stopped, his face only inches away from hers. 'I would have thought Mitchell Fraser's daughter would value honesty more highly.'

It was difficult to breathe when every breath brought her stomach up against his, making her conscious of every muscle and curve of his body. Her voice, when she found it, was choked. 'By honesty, I suppose you mean an admission of how attractive I find you.'

'Sexy is the word, Miss Fraser. I know I sure as hell find you sexy. Maybe it's just as well you didn't come into the pool without your suit because I feel like making passionate love to you right here and now.'

'And what you want, you take, I suppose,' she retorted. 'Very well, if it massages your ego, I'll admit I find you sexually attractive. But love and lust are two different things.'

He moved very slightly against her, enough to send shivers of desire up her spine. Her fingers fluttered at her sides like a school of minnows and finally came to rest against his back. His response was to grip her more tightly. 'Who's talking about love? I told you I was off women, totally and permanently. But that doesn't mean I can't enjoy what they have to give occasionally.'

'I'm afraid that your "love 'em and leave 'em" philosophy doesn't agree with me,' she said. 'I knew sharing a house wasn't going to work.'

'Oh, it's working very well,' he said, his tone caressing. 'In fact, we both might have a better vacation because of it.'

She became thoroughly annoyed. 'If you're proposing a nice casual fling while we're here, you can forget it. If I had any sort of feeling for you, Mister Marron, you just killed it stone dead!'

He lifted his body a fraction and she used the moment to wriggle out from under him and strike out for the far side of the pool, where she hoisted herself on to the coping. 'Whoever called you Mister Nice Guy didn't know what they were talking about!' she threw at him as she stood up. 'Now I can see why Laine Grosvenor walked out on you.'

He watched as she stalked away, annoyance in every line of her body. He wished some of his critics who said he couldn't act his way out of a paper bag had been here to witness the scene.

Coming on to Belle when he had no intention of following through was one of the toughest things he'd ever done. Even now his body throbbed with the need of her and he could still feel her nubile body under him.

But damn it, he had done the only thing he could. Since Belle was so set on staying under the same roof with him, he couldn't risk her getting any crazy ideas about them. She had already confessed to having had a crush on him as a teenager, and he suspected she wasn't over it yet. Which was the last thing he needed in his life right now, with Laine still on the warpath.

He had to smile at the thought. Belle would call it another of his conceits. Maybe, but he was positive she still felt something for him. He sure as hell felt something for her!

There was a quality about Belle which set her apart from the other women he had known. She was a good listener, for one thing. She actually heard what you were telling her, instead of waiting for an opportunity to talk about herself.

She was beautiful, no doubt about that, but she had a quality which went deeper than outward beauty. Considering her background, it was remarkable that she had remained as unspoiled and charming as she was.

Suddenly he realised he was still sitting on the steps of the pool with a silly grin on his face. Now he knew he had done the right thing, before she got to him more than she had already.

Good lord, he had come a within a hair's breadth of telling her the truth about Laine, when the whole point of paying Laine had been to stop her story going any further. It wasn't that he didn't trust Belle. He trusted her more readily than anyone else he knew. But the fewer people who knew Laine's story, the less chance there was of the media getting hold of it. It would kill his mother if they did.

All the same, he was sorely tempted to take the risk with Belle. Her contemptuous expression as she had walked away made him feel as if someone was twisting a knife in his gut. He really liked her and, under any other circumstances, it would be fantastic to explore what else he could feel for her.

Under any other circumstances, he reminded himself.

He had a momentary vision of his mother, so frighteningly pale yet still genteel in her British stoicism. As he had told Belle earlier, if it wasn't for her, he would have died in the plane crash. She was worth every penny he had paid to Laine.

Except that he hadn't counted on paying such a high price as the loss of any chance at a future with a girl like Belle Fraser.

A circle of yellow light formed around him and he looked upwards. Belle had turned on the light in her bedroom and it cast a glow over the pool.

His stomach muscles tightened as he watched her shadow move across the blind. Whether she was still in the bikini or not he couldn't say, but her breasts stood out firm and high and the curve of her hip was clearly visible in silhouette.

He sucked in his breath, thankful that he wasn't wearing swimming trunks. They would be damned uncomfortable right now, the way his body insisted on responding to Belle's nearness. God, if her shadow could do this to him, how long could he stay around her substance and still pretend to be unmoved?

With a muffled oath, he threw himself off the steps into the deeper water and began swimming towards the end of the pool with powerful, thrusting strokes.

CHAPTER FOUR

NEXT day, Belle sat at her typewriter trying to feel grateful to Rex. His suggestion that they should have a holiday affair had brought her to her senses. She didn't need distractions like that just when her writing career was about to blossom. In any case, she didn't want to exchange being in her father's shadow for being in Rex's.

So why didn't she feel grateful? Instead, she felt aroused and disturbed. Every time she remembered the slippery feel of his hard, masculine body against hers, tremors surged through her. She could recall the warmth of his hands stroking her back as if he was still caressing her.

It was just as well he had reminded her in time about his attitude towards women. 'Use 'em and lose 'em,' she said aloud, quoting a line of dialogue from one of his films. In the film, he had played a tough crime boss whose only allegiance was to himself. He had apparently taken the role to heart!

She should do the same, she told herself. Except that she couldn't use people and discard them. She'd seen too much of that in the film industry. So a casual affair with Rex was out of the question. Since there was no future for them and she couldn't settle for using or being used, that was an end to it.

Or so her mind accepted. Unfortunately, her body refused to be a party to the deal and she kept having sudden surges of quivery feeling, just when she thought all her attention was on her work.

Almost of their own volition, her feet slipped back into her sandals and she rose, moving like a sleepwalker out to the terrace.

Rex was there as she had known he was. Her breathing quickened at the sight of his lean body stretched out on a sun lounger. He was wearing only the briefest swimming trunks and the sun glinted off his honeyed skin.

He was reading a script held with both hands in front of his chest. One leg, corded with muscles, was stretched out on the lounger and the other dangled over the side. He looked so magnificent that she stood for several minutes, drinking in the sight of him as she might admire a Rodin sculpture at an exhibition.

Then he moved, shattering the spell. 'Hello,' he said in that marvellously rich voice. 'How long have you been standing there?'

'Not long.' She felt an urge to explain her need to be here. 'I . . . er . . . got a bit cramped sitting at the desk and needed some fresh air.'

He treated her to one of his devastating lop-sided grins which had endeared him to millions of film-goers. 'No need to explain. I think I got the best deal on offices.'

He swung his legs to the tiles and patted the sun lounger. 'Come and join me for a spell.'

'If you're sure I'm not interrupting anything.'

He grimaced at the script still held in one hand. 'This deserves an Oscar for the worst screenplay in fifty years.' He gestured towards a pile of scripts on the tiles near his feet. 'And it's the best of what I've read this morning.'

'Nothing promising?' she asked as she dropped on to the lounger beside him. Even with a foot of space between them she could feel the heat emanating from his sun-warmed body.

'Yes,' he drawled. 'There is one property I've read since coming here which shows promise.'

'And that is?'

'Your book.'

She felt a tidal wave of heat rush to her face. 'You haven't read my book?'

'After you went to bed last night. It was lying beside the typewriter, and you didn't tell me not to look at it.'

Oh, God! All the closeness she had denied herself, since Ted, had been allowed her characters—and Rex had read it all. It was an effort to keep her tone neutral when her heart was racing double-time. 'What did you think of my book?'

'The story is a bit clichéd, but the characters fairly leap off the pages at you. I shouldn't mind playing Rafe in a movie version at all.'

Now she understood. All along, she had created the character of Rafe Telstar with Rex Marron in mind. Her teenage crush had matured into a full-blown love affair from a distance and she had poured out all her longing for him into Rafe's scenes. No wonder they rang true. She was horrified that it had taken her until now to realise what was going on.

She hoped Rex hadn't recognised himself, and the depth of her feelings for him. 'I really had a younger man in mind,' she said carefully. It was partly true. Rex had been much younger when she had first met him.

'I see. Who did you have in mind for Sapphire?'

Herself, but she couldn't let him see that. Otherwise it wouldn't take him long to put two and two together and realise that her love for him had endured since her teens. What a laugh that would give to a man who only believed in one-night stands!

So far she had managed to conceal it from herself. Could she keep it from him? She shrugged. 'I don't know—an actress like Laine Grosvenor, I suppose.'

His eyes narrowed in annoyance at the thinly veiled barb, but his voice was level when he spoke. 'Much too hard-boiled. Sapphire is a child of a new world, an innocent who is wide open to Rafe's brand of charm.'

It was an accurate assessment, but she couldn't say so without giving her own feelings away. She wasn't about to do that, knowing how Rex felt about getting involved with any woman after Laine.

'Her character could change,' she suggested. 'The book is still in first draft.'

'That would be a pity,' he said softly. Imperceptibly, his body swayed towards her and she found herself drawn in his direction.

At once she jumped up. 'I have to get back to work.'

His eyes danced with mocking laughter. 'Whatever you say—Sapphire.'

She fled back to her office. He knew! All along, he had known that Sapphire was a thinly disguised version of herself—so he must know that Rafe was really Rex Marron. She had written the story of their love affair as she would have liked it to be. But Rex had made it clear that the kind of commitment she'd given to Rafe was not for him, not any more.

For two people who were supposed to be keeping their distance, they found a lot of reasons to be in each other's company, Rex thought as he made fresh coffee for them both.

First she came to him by the pool, using the excuse that she needed the air. Since her study boasted wide french doors opening on to the terrace, she didn't really need to go as far as the pool.

Then later he found he needed to visit her office to check some reference books. The ensuing discussion over word meanings was totally unnecessary, but gave them another excuse to spend time together.

Damn it, she was beginning to get under his skin. He had intended to frighten her off by telling her he'd read her manuscript, but it hadn't worked. She was right when she said he was too mature to play Rafe, but he was convinced she was the role model for Sapphire, so who was Rafe?

He had no reason to be concerned, but the question nagged at him. To his annoyance, he found that he cared.

She came into the kitchen, interrupting his thoughts. 'Oh good, coffee. I was just coming to make some.'

He smiled involuntarily, enjoying the sight of her clad in cut-off denims and a linen shirt. The top buttons had slipped open, and he tried hard not to picture the inviting cleft which was partly revealed. 'I must have read your mind.'

She blanched, hoping to God that he hadn't. If he had, he would have seen how rapidly her body responded to his presence. She grew warm at the sight of him and her pulses quickened. He was like a drug she couldn't get out of her system.

She had lied when she said she was coming to make coffee. In truth, she'd heard him pottering around the kitchen and had been drawn to the room as if on an invisible lead.

She had just finished editing a particularly torrid passage where Rafe finally made love to his space maiden, and her body quivered with sympathetic arousal. Finding Rex in the kitchen was like walking into the book and taking part in one of her own scenes. Unfortunately, she wasn't as adept as Sapphire at finding the right words to say to him.

She settled for, 'How's it going?'

'The scripts aren't getting any better,' he said with a grimace. 'How are Rafe and Sapphire getting on?'

It was out before she could stop it. 'In bed together.'

He grinned. 'I'm glad at least one of us is having an interesting day.'

Well, at least he hadn't suggested they rehearse some of the scenes from the book, she thought with a flood of relief. The tension in the air between them was already palpable. Goodness knew what ideas Rex had formed about her from reading the manuscript. She wouldn't like to give him any more food for thought.

He seemed to sense her apprehension. 'I think we could both use some air. Why don't we take a break for a while and go for a walk?'

'How does that fit in with our agreement?' she asked. 'You know—separate vacations and all that?'

'I don't see any problem. We could take separate walks and just happen to go the same way.'

He had a point, and she was ready for some exercise. She decided to take his idea at face value. 'All right, you're on.'

Even though she had spent the morning telling herself there was no point in getting involved with him, she got ready for the walk with enthusiasm. It was only that she was looking forward to the exercise, she told herself firmly.

All the same she took more than usual care in her choice of a cotton divided skirt and flame-coloured halter top which wrapped snugly over her full breasts. Lavishing sunscreen over her exposed skin, she donned a wide-brimmed straw hat and bounded out on to the terrace.

He eyed her outfit with approval. 'Very nice. But you didn't have to go to so much trouble on my account.'

'It wasn't on your account,' she said stiffly, annoyed because he was right. 'I dress to please myself.'

'Then maybe you should wear a bra next time,' he snapped back and set off across the beach at a brisk pace.

She caught up with him quickly. 'Jut a minute. I'm on holiday here too, remember? Sometimes a woman gets tired of wearing a bra. Why do men always have to think we're out to trap them when we dress for comfort?'

'Because you usually are,' was his terse rejoinder.

As they walked across the fiery sand, the brisk movement drained some of the tension away, so the mood was much more relaxed by the time they rounded a headland where Belle intended to go reef-walking.

'Have you been on the Reef before?' she asked as they approached the coral ledge which was visible at low tide.

'Not here on Mana Island, but I've been to Lizard and Heron Islands,' he explained.

Some imp of mischief made her ask, 'With the jet set, I suppose?'

He crooked an eyebrow at her. 'As a matter of fact, I prefer them because they're unspoiled. On Lizard, I'm left to myself and on Heron, I can enjoy the birdlife and the turtle colonies.'

Which fitted in with his Mister Nice Guy image, she conceded. Or at least, the way he used to be. After his unsubtle approaches last night and his teasing today, she doubted whether the label still applied.

Nevertheless, he seemed determined to prove her wrong by being courteous and charming for the rest of their walk. Since she knew the island so well, he let her take the lead and listened intently as she pointed out natural features she thought might interest him.

At low tide, they reached a small inlet where fingers of coral reached to just below the surface of the water, creating channels of delicate green shading to darker blue where the coral fell away towards the ocean.

Picking their way with care, they ventured out on to the coral runways, admiring the staghorns, brain corals and mushroom corals growing just beneath the surface. They were interwoven with the waving fields of soft coral, colourful anemones and shellfish which clung to the Reef.

'I'm glad I brought my snorkelling gear,' Rex said after a while.

'If you like to dive, there's a wonderful pool here which has easy access to the deeper water.'

'You dive, too?' he asked in surprise.

'Shouldn't I?'

'I don't know, I just didn't expect it somehow.'

She could understand his surprise. Most of the starlets she knew reserved their spirit of adventure for aerobics classes, getting no closer to nature than a jungle set in Hollywood. Of course, there were a few who did try anything and everything, even doing their own stunt work. Apparently, Rex didn't know any women like that. 'Didn't Laine go diving with you?' she asked innocently.

'No,' he snapped back, giving her her answer.

She felt foolishly pleased to have one skill the beautiful Miss Grosvenor didn't possess, then chided herself. This wasn't a contest for Rex Marron's attention.

It was almost sunset when they returned to the villa. The long walk and the sea air had sharpened her appetite, so Belle headed straight for the kitchen, but Rex paused in the doorway. 'I'd better go to the store before it closes.'

'Are we out of anything?' She hadn't noticed.

'No, but I have to stock up on TV dinners, remember?'

He had remembered their deal, even if she'd forgotten. Suddenly, she didn't want him to eat alone. The idea of cooking for him had become oddly appealing. 'You can forget the TV dinners,' she said heavily. 'I'll do the cooking and you can do the cleaning up. Fair enough?'

The corners of his mouth turned upwards and she caught a glimpse of perfect white teeth. Her breathing quickened. Being caught in the glow of his smile was like being under a sun-lamp. 'It's a deal,' he confirmed.

'But nothing else has changed,' she cautioned, disturbed by the intensity of her response to his smile.

'Of course not,' he agreed solemnly.

If they were still having strictly separate holidays, how come he took every excuse to drop into the kitchen while she was cooking? she wondered uneasily. Then there was the coffee break this afternoon and the invitation to go reef-walking with him. What was he up to?

'I'm not up to anything,' he said in an aggrieved tone, when she brought the question up over dinner. 'Have I made one untoward move towards you today?'

'No,' she conceded unwillingly. Most of his advances had been in her own mind.

'Have I interfered with your work?'

'No.'

'Then how can you say I'm not sticking to our agreement?'

She twisted her table napkin into a rope. 'I don't know. Maybe it's just having you around. You're...you're a distraction,' she said triumphantly.

He scraped his chair back from the table. 'So now I'm a distraction, am I? What am I supposed to be—the invisible man?'

'I didn't mean to hurt you. I suppose I was counting on having the place to myself, that's all.'

'For that matter, so was I, and I'm not complaining because you distract me.'

This was something she hadn't considered. 'Do I?' she asked. 'Distract you, I mean?' The idea was curiously attractive and her pulses picked up speed as she waited for his answer.

'You know damned well you do,' he growled. 'I must have been crazy to think we could stay here together and keep everything platonic, especially with you swanning around in that skin-tight top and no bra.'

Her temper flared. 'Now it's all my fault! I'll bet you're the kind of man who, when a girl is raped, assumes she was asking for it.'

'Only if she goes around in man-trap clothing and expects men to be made of stone.'

It was so unfair that she didn't stop to think. She crossed the floor in quick strides, her arm upraised before she reached him.

His response was faster. He grabbed her arm and forced it back to her side. 'I warn you, lady,' he said through gritted teeth, 'you slap me, and I'll slap you back so hard your senses will reel.'

They were already reeling, but with the effect of his nearness, more than any threat. 'I wasn't...' she began.

'You were going to hit me, admit it.'

'All right, I was, but you were asking for it.'

Feeling the tension go out of her, he released her and she clutched the kitchen counter for support. 'What's happening to me?' she asked in horror. 'I've shared a house with other people before—men and women—and never acted like this.'

'Probably because they didn't mean anything to you,' he observed tautly.

'And you do, I suppose?'

'Face it, Belle, we're about as strongly attracted to each other as two people can be. Call it chemistry, or what you will. I can feel it and I'm certain you can.'

She could hardly force the words out through parched lips. 'Yes, I can feel it.'

'Then I'm right in assuming I'm Rafe to your Sapphire?'

'Yes.'

'Damn!'

This was hardly the reaction she had expected. 'I gather you don't welcome the discovery,' she said stiffly.

It was the last thing he needed, but not for the reason she assumed. Belle thought that after the lawsuit he was shy of any romantic involvement. In fact it was the opposite.

Rex yearned for intimacy with a woman. Not just the sexual kind, either. He wanted the 'marriage of true minds' that Shakespeare so aptly described. But how could he leave himself open to such a relationship knowing that Laine was there like a bird of prey, to jeopardise his plans?

The risk was too great for his mother who was so terribly vulnerable right now, and also for Belle who was vulnerable in her own way.

He made his voice hard. 'Why should I? I just got myself out of one expensive entanglement. I'd hardly be looking for another, and you already made it clear you aren't interested in any holiday high-jinks.' He grinned wickedly. 'Although the offer is still open.'

'No, thank you,' she said primly.

'Well, that leaves us with only one option. One of us has to leave.' He hefted a coin in one hand. 'I'll toss you for it.'

The corners of her mouth twitched upwards. 'You know very well why we can't, for the same reasons as before. I have no home to go to, and you can't leave the island while that news-hungry reporter is nosing around.'

He thought for a moment. 'I have another idea.'

'If it's shared beds, I already told you...'

'Whoa! I can take no for an answer. I was going to suggest we look for some crowded places where we couldn't give in to our inclinations even if we wanted to.'

'What did you have in mind?' she asked suspiciously.

'There must be some tourist attractions on this island. Surely it isn't entirely fenced off for the benefit of the rich and famous?'

'No-o,' she said thoughtfully. 'The fences stop about half-way across the island. Then there's a belt of National Parkland and a few tourist attractions on the far side. Not that many visitors come here, mind you. There's only one ferry a day from the mainland which arrives around eleven and takes the day trippers back around three.'

'Perfect. We can sightsee until the boat comes in, then hide out in a restaurant for lunch until they leave.'

She nodded agreement. 'It would solve the problem of you being recognised,' she observed. 'The islanders themselves are so used to famous people coming and going that it's considered gross to stare.'

'Then it's settled. We keep our distance tonight and make like harmless tourists tomorrow. All right with you?'

She doubted whether he could ever be called harmless, and certainly not where her hormones were concerned, but she inclined her head. At least he couldn't sweep her off her feet in a crowd.

Somehow she got through a restless night, ach-ingly aware that he was sleeping only a few doors

away. Next day she joined him at breakfast, armed
with booklets about the island. 'Dad keeps these
for house guests,' she explained. 'They're a little
out of date, but the attractions themselves haven't
changed.'

' "Two shillings admission to the underwater observatory". I'll bet the prices have changed,' he
teased.

She threw a folder at him. 'I said they were old
brochures.'

After more good-natured bantering, they settled
on a visit to the underwater marine observatory, a
steel tank sunk into the coral bed. Here, one could
view the many species of fish living along the Reef,
as well as the splendidly coloured coral and giant
clams which opened cavernous jaws in search of
food.

'Sounds like some of the producers I know,' Rex
quipped when she read this part out.

He was a different person this morning, Belle
thought as she drove carefully along the winding
track which traversed the National Park and led to
the far side of the island. He seemed distant
somehow. Last night's closeness might have been
a figment of her imagination.

In fact he had spent most of the night schooling
himself into his present mood. It wasn't easy with
Belle sitting shoulder-to-thigh alongside him in her
compact car. It was an electric vehicle not much
larger than a golf cart, but was ideal for scooting
around the small island.

He wasn't a car snob, but he would have preferred a front seat which put a little more space between them. Then he wouldn't have been so aware of her body heat and the sensuous message in her every movement as she manoeuvred the car. It played havoc with the devil-may-care demeanour he had spent the night perfecting in a fit of Stanislavsky zeal.

Luckily the drive was short. In less than half an hour they were pulling up outside the glassed-in entrance to the observatory. 'Here we are,' Belle announced.

While she parked the car, he purchased their tickets, noting wryly that the two-shilling admission had grown to five dollars each.

It would have been value at twice the price, he decided, when they climbed down the steel staircase into the immense chamber which effectively reversed the man-and-fishbowl roles.

For over an hour they watched the underwater spectacle in fascination. If Belle noticed when Rex slid an arm around her shoulders to point out some new sight, she said nothing, but her breathing was noticeably quickened and he was aware of a slight tremor under his fingers.

Since the tourist boat hadn't yet arrived, they had the place to themselves. Before their wondering eyes, giant clams opened their mantles and strained the Reef waters for microscopic food. At one time, millions of sardine-like fish gathered near the portholes, only to be scattered by shoals of mackerel and trevally, eager for their breakfast.

'What does it remind you of?' Rex asked her.

She made a *moue* of distaste. 'A casting call.'

Laughing, they moved from one viewing porthole to another, feasting their eyes on the Reef's beauty. When Rex spotted some exquisite star-shaped flowers set into skeletons of limestone, she explained that the flowerlike animals, small as they were, were the very creatures out of which all twelve hundred miles of the Great Barrier Reef was built.

Rex whistled appreciatively. 'No wonder they call this the world's largest living thing. It must have taken all of time to grow here.'

'It's still growing,' she reminded him, then glanced at her watch. 'And speaking of time, shouldn't we get out of here before the day trippers arrive?'

Reluctantly he tore his gaze from the windows. 'You're right. Let's go eat.'

There were two restaurants on the island, one so prohibitively expensive that few of the tourists went there, preferring the less costly bistro attached to a small guest house nearby. Poisson d'Or suited their needs admirably.

'Nice place,' Rex observed, looking around at the prettily contrived island décor. Let into the walls were a series of glass tanks filled with tropical fish, a pleasing reminder of the observatory. 'I hope that isn't the menu,' Rex said, gesturing towards the tanks.

'Relax, they're all protected species,' she assured him, 'all except those.'

He followed her pointing finger to a vast tank in the centre of the room. It was filled with greenish-blue crayfish, climbing over one another in a tangle of legs and tentacles.

He grinned. 'You say they aren't protected?' When she shook her head, he turned to the waiter. 'Lobster mornay for two, thanks.'

They declined the waiter's invitation to choose their own victims, and settled down to devour huge platters of plump rock oysters while their lobster was being prepared.

'This is almost sinful,' Belle said, squeezing lemon juice over her shellfish.

'Not as sinful as what we'd be doing if we hadn't come here.'

It was the first provocative thing he'd said to her all day, and she darted a disturbed glance. 'I thought we called a truce?'

'Not a truce, diversionary tactics,' he amended. 'Nothing has changed.'

A sensation of longing surged through her and she bit her lower lip to control it. 'For me, neither,' she agreed.

He was telling her that he was still only interested in a one-night fling and, since she wasn't, it remained at stalemate. She felt curiously disappointed. But what had she expected? That a shared meal and an hour of watching the fish feed would have assuaged the hunger they felt for each other? She should have known better.

Her disappointment must have shown on her face. 'Is something wrong with your shellfish?' he asked.

She speared another forkful of the luscious meat. 'No, it's perfect, thank you.'

What a shame there wasn't a recipe for a successful love affair, she thought as she ate. Take a portion of man and a serving of woman and a *soupçon* of caring, add a dash of passion and *voilà*! *'Two souls bonne femme',* she mentally christened the dish. Except that it was never so simple. Love was too unpredictable: sweet one minute and sour the next.

'You're very quiet,' he commented. 'What are you thinking about?'

'Cooking,' she answered truthfully, and hoped he wouldn't press her for details.

But his attention was diverted by the arrival of a noisy group of people. The waiters bustled around, rearranging tables to accommodate them. 'Oh no,' Rex groaned, ducking his head.

'Someone you know?'

'All of them. Sammy Durant, the short, stout man, is a producer. Frank Bright is a director of photography and the rest are actors I've worked with once or twice.'

She understood his dismay. 'A film crew! They must be here to work. Unless...you don't think they're just visiting, do you?' she asked hopefully.

'No way. Two of those actors wouldn't be seen in each other's company unless they were on someone's payroll.' He gestured for their bill. 'Let's get out of here before they spot us.'

But it was too late. The man Rex had identified as Sammy Durant was already coming up to them, his round face wreathed in smiles. 'Well, fancy meeting you here, Rex, my boy!'

Rex looked around anxiously but no one was listening. He drew Sammy on to a seat beside them. 'Keep it down, Sammy, I'm here incognito.'

'I see.' He looked curiously at Belle. 'Are you the reason for the secrecy?'

'No,' said Rex firmly. 'Belle Fraser is my hostess. She's Mitchell Fraser's daughter. He and I are old friends.'

Sammy regarded her with new respect. 'I thought I'd seen you around the traps. I worked with your father on his last mini-series. How is he?'

'Fine, thanks. He's in London at the moment, doing Shakespeare for British television.'

Sammy rolled his eyes. 'Ah, the dream of every thespian! I'm afraid the stuff we're doing isn't nearly as lofty as that.'

'What are you doing?' Rex asked.

'A feature called *Hibiscus Coast*. It's a thriller with a South Pacific background.'

He had confirmed their worst fears. 'You're here on location?' Belle stated rather than asked.

Sammy frowned. 'We're supposed to be. I was told there were mangrove swamps here. I *need* mangrove swamps. But my location scouts screwed up. All I see here are beaches and palm trees.'

'The mangroves are on the other side of the island, beside Mana Colony,' Belle said tiredly, then could have bitten her tongue off when she saw Sammy's immediate look of interest.

'On the other side, really? Then we haven't blown the budget, after all. Can you direct me to these mangroves?'

'Not really, they're on private property,' she dissembled.

'Then introduce me to the owner. I'll offer him any price, just so we can get these blasted scenes in the can.'

Belle felt as if someone was piling weights on top of her head to see how many it would take before she disappeared in the sand up to her knees. She could deny any knowledge of the owner but it wouldn't take Sammy Durant long to find out the truth. Anyone on the island would tell him who owned the stretch of mangroves he coveted. And a man like him would give her little peace until he got his own way.

'I don't have to introduce you,' she said in a defeated voice. 'You're looking at her.'

CHAPTER FIVE

IN Belle's study, the green-painted wooden shutters filtered the late afternoon sun and captured the cool sea breezes, but did not shut out the clamour of voices and activity going on not far from the villa.

'Get those Kleigs over here.'

'Make-up! Where the devil is make-up?'

'Somebody mask those power-lines with fake palm leaves.'

Listening to it all, Belle pushed aside the manuscript pages she'd been trying to edit. As if on cue, Rex walked in, two glasses of iced coffee in hand.

He gave one to her. 'Awful, isn't it? I couldn't get any work done, either.' Dropping into the seat opposite her desk, he hooked one tanned leg over the arm. 'You know, when I suggested we surround ourselves with people in order to ward off the inevitable, I didn't mean you to go quite so far.'

'I know. It wasn't what I had in mind when I came to the island, either. But what could I do? Once Sammy Durant found out that the mangroves he needed were on Dad's property he got straight on the phone to London. You have Mitchell Fraser to thank for giving the crew the freedom of the colony.'

'Your father always was the hospitable type.'

She was tempted to remind him that if it wasn't for her father's renowned hospitality, he wouldn't be here and the problem wouldn't have arisen in the first place. As she held her tongue with an effort, Rex guessed what she was thinking.

'I have rather messed up your vacation, haven't I?' he asked.

'Working holiday,' she amended. 'Not that I'm getting much of either—holiday or work—done.'

His gaze went to the pile of manuscript pages in front of her. 'How's it going?'

'I'm nearly finished, thank goodness. If Durant and his team had arrived when I was just starting my editing, I'd have gone crazy. As it is, I'll settle for mildly insane.'

Rex drained his drink and set the glass down, then uncoiled in a lazy movement from his chair. 'Come on.'

'Come on where?'

'If you can't beat 'em, join 'em. Let's see what the film crew is up to. I'm curious, even if you aren't.'

She was, but she hadn't wanted to admit it, trying instead to maintain her aloofness all morning. Now she was only too glad to accompany Rex out to the clearing on the edge of the mangrove swamps, where Sammy and his team were working.

Mitchell had given them unlimited use of the grounds, inviting Sammy and the principals to stay in the guest wing of the villa. The rest of the crew were staying in the guest house on the other side of the island.

With no housekeeper in residence, Belle had made it clear that anyone staying in the villa would have to do their own housework. Mitchell was entitled to do what he liked with his property, but that didn't include her services.

'Well, at least I know the problem isn't me,' Rex had commented when she finished giving her 'welcome, but' speech.

'What do you mean?' she asked, genuinely puzzled.

'You've just made it clear to the film crew that your services aren't part of Mitchell's hospitality. I was beginning to think your touch-me-not attitude was strictly directed at me.'

'Let's say you gave me the idea,' she retorted. 'As it was, Dad was astonished to find I'd been living here for weeks. God knows what he made of you being here as well.'

'But you told him we were—quote—"just good friends"?' Rex mused.

'I told him we're not *even* good friends,' she rejoined. 'In fact, I told him what I thought of him sending you here unannounced.'

Rex seemed unperturbed. 'And?'

She was forced to tell the truth. 'And he laughed. Said it might do me some good to have a man like you around for a while.'

'Do you think it will?'

Her anger flared like a rocket going off. 'Why do men always think women are incomplete without them?'

Rex was at her side in an instant, twisting her to face him. 'Now just a minute! Save your hostility for someone who deserves it. I had a perfect right to come here, and if it didn't suit you there was nobody stopping you from leaving. I'm not trying to run your life, so there's no need to take your anger against your father out on me. What I feel for you is anything but fatherly. Why do you think I've been fighting it so hard since I got here?'

All right, so he was attracted to her, wanted her. She felt the same way. They had already acknowledged that what they felt was pure sexual chemistry, so she was being unfair in attacking him.

'I'm sorry,' she said, deflating. 'I guess I'm uptight about the way my father thinks he knows what's best for me. I tend to suspect any man's motives, but you've already made yours plain.'

His hold on her arm relaxed, but he kept his fingers curled around her quivering skin. 'I'm glad you understand my motives, Belle. With you in my arms like this, I could sweep you off to the bedroom without another thought. And I think you'd come, too.'

Her lips felt dry and she moistened them with a darting tongue which made his breathing quicken. Not trusting herself to speak, she nodded imperceptibly. The desire she felt for Rex dated back to their first encounter, but had been masked then by her teenage hostility. Now she was a woman and she recognised her feelings for what they were. But she was determined not to give in to them and become another butterfly in his collection.

Sensing her resolve, Rex released her. She glanced at her upper arm and noted the fast-fading outlines of his fingers against her tanned skin. His grip had been compelling. It would take so little to give in and go with him ... and what would be, would be.

'No, it wouldn't work, would it?' Rex said in a tone of regret. 'I'm off limits to women now, at least on a permanent basis, and you won't accept anything less, will you?'

At that moment she would have given almost anything to be able to say the future didn't matter, that she would gladly be his for one night, or as many as he was offering.

He hadn't referred to that scene when they had met this morning for breakfast, but she knew it was on his mind from the tender, regretful way he looked at her as she prepared their omelettes and squeezed oranges for juice.

Had his sleep been as fragmented as hers, disturbed by phantom longings and surges of searing heat which came and went with frightening intensity? She almost hoped it had. He had destroyed her peace of mind. It was only fair that he should suffer equally for it.

Now, as he led the way past the pool to the mangrove-fringed beach, she was impressed anew by the breadth of his shoulders in the figure-skimming gauze shirt which revealed every muscle and contour to her searching gaze.

Under the shirt, his white shorts hugged his strong thighs as if they had been painted on. With each long stride, the corded muscles of his legs stood out and his sandalled feet etched deep prints in the beach.

Childishly, she began to step in his prints, and found that her legs, long as they were, had to stretch to link one print with another. She gave up the game, annoyed with herself for being foolish, and hurried to catch up with him.

'Will Sammy mind having an audience?' she asked, a little out of breath with trying to match his strides.

'You name me the director who doesn't enjoy an audience, especially when it's one of our own,' he said drily.

He was right. A few directors closed their sets to all but actors and crew, putting professionalism before everything else. But just as many directors adored having an audience of appreciative fellow film-makers, to 'ooh' and 'ah' over every masterful touch. She wondered which type Sammy Durant was.

They found the director on the edge of the mangrove swamp, supervising the setting up of a master scene. The actors she'd seen at the restaurant were there, along with several extras. All were made up as island natives. 'Headhunters?' she laughed, taking in the fierce war-paint.

'From what Sammy's told me of the plot, the hero and heroine crash land on an uncharted island which turns out to be inhabited by a lost tribe of— you guessed it—headhunters.'

'Sounds like a lot of fun,' she agreed.

Sammy noticed them and came over. 'I've promised Mitch that we won't harm any of the flora and fauna,' he assured them.

'I know you won't. That isn't why we're here. We just couldn't resist poking our noses in,' she confessed.

Sammy nodded. 'I'm the same. Even on vacation, I'm drawn to a film set like a magnet. I guess we've got the bug, that's all.'

He swung around to initial some sheets handed to him by a continuity girl, then frowned. 'Why isn't Lisa here? This is her big scene. She's the girl queen of the lost tribe,' he explained to Rex and Belle. 'She's only in a handful of scenes, all of them shot here, but she's vital to the storyline.'

'I'm afraid you'll have to find yourself another girl queen,' the cameraman, Frank Bright, said as he came panting up to them. 'Lisa's just collapsed in Make-up.'

'Oh God, now what?'

They followed Sammy to the tent which had been set up as a make-up and wardrobe centre. Lisa, still in her native girl costume, lay doubled up on a camp stretcher.

'Has somebody sent for a doctor?' Sammy demanded.

'There's one staying at the guest house. He's on his way over,' a make-up girl explained.

'What is it, Lisa, something you ate?' Sammy asked the groaning girl.

She shook her head. 'No, it's nothing like that.'

'Then what, for goodness' sake? A tropical bug of some kind?'

The girl screwed her eyes tight shut. 'I wish it was, then it would be cured in less than nine months.'

Sammy's gaze cleared. 'Nine months? You mean, you're pregnant? Oh Lisa, how could you do this to me?'

'To you? I'm the one having the baby. I thought I'd be all right to complete my scenes, but I didn't expect to feel so ill all the time.'

She must be one of those women who were laid low for most of their pregnancy, Belle thought.

At her insistence, they helped the girl into the villa and settled her on a comfortable bed while they waited for the doctor to return. When he arrived, he confirmed that nothing was amiss, but that Lisa would have to get a lot more rest—which meant giving up work right away, or risk losing the baby.

'So where does that leave me?' Sammy said as they consoled him with a drink in the villa. 'My lead actress arrives tomorrow and there's no supporting lead to play opposite her.' Suddenly he set the glass down and stared at Belle. 'Unless...'

Guessing what he was thinking, Belle shook her head emphatically. 'No, you don't. I'm no jungle queen.'

'But you are an actress and a paid-up member of Equity. And you are here, on the spot.'

'And a damned good actress,' Rex chimed in.

She shot him a startled glance. 'How would you know?'

'After you confessed who you were, I rifled through your father's videotape collection and found some of your TV films. Even though they were all small parts, you made the most of them.'

'There, you see,' Sammy said triumphantly as if the matter was settled.

'I don't see anything,' she cried. 'I came here to finish a book, not to get involved in ... in ...'

'You may as well say it,' Sammy said heavily. 'A two-bit picture like this one.'

'I didn't say any such thing.'

'But you were thinking it.' He stood up. 'Very well, I won't take up any more of your writing time. I'd better go and give the cast the bad news.'

After the director left, Rex looked at her accusingly. 'You were awfully rough on the poor guy.'

'I didn't say anything about his picture. He put the words in my mouth,' she defended herself. 'How come you're so keen to see me take the part?'

'Now you're putting words in my mouth. I didn't say I wanted you to do it. I said you're a damned good actress and I stand by that. Sammy Durant is also a first-rate director. If he says this picture is worth doing, then you can be sure it is.'

'So everybody has a say in this except me,' she said petulantly.

'Now you really are being stupid. What can it possibly hurt to do a few scenes as a favour to Sammy? He's been good to your father in his turn, so you'd be pleasing Mitch. And let's face it, you would be pleasing yourself, too.'

She regarded him suspiciously. 'In what way?'

'You wanted a way to put some distance between us until I return to the mainland. What better way than to be on the set of a movie every day till I leave?'

'Are you saying you'll go as soon as the film is completed?'

'If having my promise will help you decide to do the picture, then all right, I promise.'

It sounded too good to be true. 'You'll really let me have the villa to myself?'

'If it's what you want. I realise we aren't doing each other any good as we are. Every time I'm in the same room with you, all I can think about is taking you to bed. It isn't conducive to getting much work done.'

She laughed in spite of herself, for she felt exactly the same way. Perhaps he was right. If she immersed herself in the filming she would save herself being tempted by Rex's disturbing presence. Because she was sure that she wouldn't be able to resist him for much longer if they continued as they were.

She hated to admit it, but she was also flattered by what he'd said about her acting. Most people saw only that she was Mitchell Fraser's daughter, as if her genes alone were responsible for any talent she possessed. Rex seemed prepared to give her at least some of the credit.

'I'll do it,' she told Sammy when she caught up with him outside the villa.

His dejected expression was replaced by one of gratitude. 'You will? What made you change your mind?'

'Rex just convinced me what a terrific director you are. I couldn't pass up the chance to work with you,' she said, her eyes sparkling with challenging humour.

'You did go to Ireland on your last holiday, didn't you?' Sammy asked with seeming irrelevance.

'Once, years ago, but . . .'

'And you kissed the Blarney Stone, of course.'

'Oh!' She was going to like working with him, after all, and she would have to watch his quick wit. Already he had proved he could give as good as he got.

In spite of her assurances to Sammy, she knew he wasn't the reason why she had agreed to take over the part. Rex wanted her to do it, and for some crazy reason that was enough. She felt a mad urge to vindicate his faith in her acting ability. Taking over a part at short notice would surely do that.

Then what? Would he see in her the kind of woman it was worth breaking his resolution for? Maybe he would decide that a permanent relationship wasn't so terrible after all. If there was a future for them, she would feel free to indulge the torrent of sensations she experienced whenever he was around. She could finally admit her love for him!

Her footsteps slowed to a halt and she sat down on the sand abruptly. Whatever was she thinking of? Using the film to demonstrate to Rex that they not only could, but should, have a future together! It was crazy. But it just might work.

She hummed to herself as she studied the lines of dialogue the jungle queen had to say to the visitors from the sky. Most of her scenes were action sequences, so the only time she needed to talk was when she confronted the strangers in the jungle.

The pilot would be played by one of the actors she'd met in the restaurant previously. The actress playing the journalist who crashed with him would arrive by helicopter next morning.

Belle began to wonder who her opposite number might be. Sammy was deep in the jungle-cum-mangrove swamp, overseeing some stunt sequences involving very dead, stuffed crocodiles and much wrestling in the mud, so she wouldn't have a chance to ask him until later in the day.

'Me Tarzan, you Jane,' came a carrying voice.

She looked up, smiling involuntarily as Rex walked into the study. 'Me not Jane, me Lara, jungle queen,' she amended, deepening her voice to match his.

'You sound as if you're enjoying yourself, your Highness,' he teased.

'I am. In spite of everything, I enjoy acting. If only I could have been plain Jane Doe instead of "Mitchell Fraser's daughter", everything would have been different.'

'It might not have been,' he reminded her. 'Sometimes, having a famous relative can ensure you get breaks you don't otherwise get. Talent isn't everything in this business. There are lots of acting geniuses pumping gas in LA.'

'You're right, of course,' she conceded. 'But I've had this hang-up about Dad for so long, it's hard to know how to get rid of it.'

'How about just letting it go? The past is past, we can't change it by fretting over it. All we can do is resolve to be different in future.'

'My, aren't we philosophical?' she mocked. 'Is that why you came in, to give me a pep talk?'

The truth was, he had come in because he couldn't stop himself, but he wasn't admitting that. Belle Fraser drew him like a magnet. It was almost impossible to concentrate on anything, knowing she was in the next room.

It was just as well she'd agreed to take the part before she tempted him to break his vow not to get seriously involved with any woman. The threat was definitely there; the very reason he should avoid it at all costs. If Laine found out, she might make good her threat against his mother and Belle would be caught in the crossfire. He didn't intend to expose her to such a risk.

He sighed heavily. 'Actually, I came to make sure you aren't sorry I talked you into doing the film.'

'You didn't. I talked myself into it,' she admitted honestly. 'I decided you're right. I shouldn't turn my back on half of what I am just because of some stupid hang-up about living in Dad's shadow. It would be different if I hated acting, but I don't.'

'I'm glad, because you have a lot of talent.'

His praise washed over her like a caress. She was more than ever convinced that she could use the picture to show him how foolish he was, avoiding entanglements.

Now he had relaxed, believing the film would keep them apart, he wouldn't be so wary of her. It shouldn't take much to turn the attraction they shared into the kind of lasting commitment that she now knew she wanted more than anything.

'Would you ever marry an actress, Rex?' she asked casually.

His response was automatic. 'I doubt it.'

'Why not?'

A vision of Laine rose before him, demanding and ruthless, making his response icy. 'Because in my experience they're self-centred, scheming and unscrupulous, and never mind who gets hurt.'

His response wounded her, although he seemed to be looking deep inside himself when he made it. She hated to think he cast her in the same ugly light and her retort came swiftly, 'I didn't want this part, remember?'

He came back to her with a seeming effort. 'But you're...' He had been going to say, 'You're different,' but he realised in time just how revealing this would be. Instead, he said, 'You're not the selfish type.'

Wasn't she? she asked herself unhappily. She had only agreed to take the part because Rex wanted her to. By dazzling him with her talent, she hoped to make him see her in a new light, as a possible future partner for himself. Now she wondered if she was doing the right thing. The only reason Rex wanted her in the film was to keep her occupied while he enjoyed an uncomplicated vacation. And he said women were selfish!

But she was committed to the film now and it wasn't in her nature to let anyone down. Still, remembering how tranquil the colony had been before the film crew arrived, she occasionally wished she had let them leave after Lisa had collapsed. Sammy couldn't have afforded to pay the cast and crew to sit around while he found a replacement actress, so they would have gone by now. She and Rex would have the villa to themselves again, the very situation Rex made it clear he wanted to avoid at all costs.

With a resigned sigh, she picked up her script and walked out.

The crew were setting up on the edge of the mangrove swamps. The trees were well christened, deriving their name from an earlier term, mangle groves. The thick, corded roots bent and twisted over and around one another as they sought oxygen above the flat, boggy sand. In between the spear-shaped leaves grew spectacular native orchids and the tuberous ant-house plants which could spill thousands of biting ants on to the arms of anyone foolish enough to break open a tuber.

'I hope we don't have to go in there,' she said to Sammy.

'Relax, honey. This is strictly a backdrop. The stunt people will take care of the 'forging through the jungle' scenes. They're insured for that sort of thing—you aren't.'

'Thank goodness for that!'

She listened carefully as Sammy explained the morning's scene in which the jungle queen and her followers found the first signs of intruders on their island. A stage hand was already stamping his way across the swept sand, leaving a trail of well defined footprints.

'When do we get to meet the intruders?' she asked Sammy gleefully. In the script, the jungle queen got to scream her head off when she was picked up and thrown over the pilot's shoulder. Her rescue provided an exciting climax to the film.

'Not until tomorrow,' Sammy told her. 'We're just doing the hunt sequence today. The capture is down for tomorrow, after our leading lady gets here.'

Now was her chance to find out more about the star. 'I've been meaning to ask you about her,' she said, surprised that he hadn't already volunteered the information.

She soon found out why he had been reluctant to tell her. He handed her a call sheet and she ran a finger down it until she came to tomorrow's cast list. Right at the top was the name, Miss Laine Grosvenor. Sammy must have known she would be less than thrilled with the discovery. It must have been obvious to anyone that she was interested in Rex Marron, and not as a house-guest either, despite Rex's glib introduction.

Suddenly she understood why Rex was so keen for her to appear in the film. It was the only way he could keep the crew around until he was reunited with Laine. Despite the much-publicised palimony suit, he must still be carrying a torch for the actress.

'Did it ever occur to you that I didn't know she was in this picture?' Rex demanded when she confronted him with the discovery.

'Do you expect me to believe that?'

'I expect you to believe the truth.'

She had considered the possibility, but discarded it, recalling how torrid things had been between Rex and Laine.

With almost no film-acting experience, she had starred in her first feature opposite Rex Marron, and the film had been a box-office smash. Another actress had been tipped to play the female lead but, presumably through Rex's intervention, the part went to Laine. The two had been an item ever since.

Not that they were often seen in public together. They avoided the glittering round of Hollywood parties and charity balls, but this only fuelled rumours that theirs was a real love-match with room for no one else.

When the news broke that Laine was moving out and suing Rex for half of everything he owned, rumours flew, but no one knew what had really happened between the former lovebirds. The case was settled out of court, disappointing the media and their peers.

'Why did you and Laine split up?' Belle asked now, thinking aloud.

His expression hardened. 'That's nobody's business but ours.'

'Are you still in love with her?'

'No comment.'

'That's hardly fair, Rex. One minute you're telling me how attractive you find me, then you're using me so you can stage a reunion with Laine Grosvenor. I have a right to know what's going on.'

This was the moment he had dreaded. Even now, as she stood confronting him, with long legs wide apart and her eyes blazing with anger, he was drawn to her as he had never been to any other woman. But dare he tell her the truth about his relationship with Laine? Only three people in the world knew the story. Belle would make four. It was already too many for comfort and he was still afraid of Laine's power over his mother—and Belle too if he wasn't careful. But still, he found himself wavering.

Belle watched the play of conflicting emotions on his even features, and a tug-of-war started up inside her. She cared so much for him that it hurt her physically to see the distress her demand had inflicted.

Suddenly she saw how unfair she was being. He had made no secret of wanting a holiday romance and nothing more, and she had turned him down. He could have been honest with her, confessing that he was still in love with Laine. But she had no right to demand explanations when they had explicitly agreed on keeping their lives separate.

Despite the justice in the thought, it took all of her courage to say, 'It's all right, Rex. I shouldn't have asked you. I don't have any claims on you, so what you do with your life is none of my business. I just hope it makes you happy.'

Before he could respond, she fled back outside to where Sammy was working. He would provide her with a diversion while she recovered her composure.

On the way she told herself it was just as well she had avoided any involvement with Rex. She could easily have given in to his request for a no-strings romance. This way, she had found out the truth in time to save herself from being hurt.

Her eyes misted over at the thought. Whom did she think she was fooling? Certainly not herself.

CHAPTER SIX

LAINE arrived by helicopter the next morning and was driven to the villa by Frank Bright, who had borrowed Belle's electric car for the purpose, unaware of the irony of his request.

The actress was to stay in the guest wing and Sammy had deputised one of the set decorators to prepare a room for her, since Belle had refused to do it.

'The deal was, you look after yourselves,' she reminded Sammy firmly. She wasn't refusing out of pique, she told herself, but if she started acting as Lady Bountiful it wouldn't be any time at all before she was expected to do all the work. Film people were the salt of the earth, but they could also be self-indulgent, using others without a second thought. Belle had been a victim of her father's whims for too many years to have any illusions on that score.

Belle wasn't sure what she expected Laine to be like, but it certainly wasn't the charming Vivien Leigh look-alike she turned out to be.

Laine was as sweet as she was pretty, and her still-strong English accent only added to her charm.

'It's so good of you to take on Lisa's part at the eleventh hour, not to mention sharing your home,' she told Belle.

'Actually, it's my father's home, and he likes nothing better than to entertain people from the industry,' she explained.

'All the same, we must be a burden on you.'

This was getting silly, Belle reflected. They were almost falling over one another to be charming. 'I'm glad we were able to help,' she said weakly.

Over the next few days as filming progressed, the crew members waited for Laine and Rex Marron to meet. It would be their first encounter since the much publicised break-up and everyone expected the fur to fly.

Belle was not sure how she felt about seeing them together. It was almost certainly the end of any involvement between her and Rex. Why else would he have gone to such pains to arrange the reunion?

For she was quite sure he had engineered it. Granted, he couldn't be blamed for Lisa leaving the cast, but he had suggested going to the underwater observatory on the very day Sammy and his crew were arriving.

Brooding about it wouldn't change anything, she sighed. She was stuck with the film now, and in spite of herself she was enjoying the part. With so much running over the sand and screaming, it was a catharsis to take part. She was becoming even more tanned and had lost a couple of pounds in weight so the jungle queen costume looked positively ravishing on her.

For all the good it would do her, she thought. How could her robust Aussie beach-girl looks ever compare with Laine's fragility which made men rush to protect her?

The crew members practically fell over themselves to fetch and carry for her. It was easy to see why Rex had succumbed to her charms.

Rex managed to avoid Laine for nearly a week, but when the two finally did meet it was almost an anticlimax. Laine and Belle were walking through a scene where the journalist was explaining flight to the jungle girl.

'We'd better go for a take. We're losing the light,' Sammy said after a while.

It was a short scene, but Laine's pantomiming was in danger of reducing Belle to helpless giggles. Only with a great effort of will, and Sammy's disapproving frown, did she pull herself together sufficiently to finish the scene.

'Cut. Print it!' Sammy called and everyone relaxed.

One of the technicians walked past Laine and imitated her pantomime of a plane in flight, then strolled off, laughing to himself.

'You wouldn't be laughing if you had to make such a fool of yourself,' Laine retorted good-naturedly. She grinned at Belle. 'I'm glad you were the one with the giggles. I was on the verge myself, but seeing the way Sammy got tough with you saved me from breaking up.'

Belle's eyes widened. It was a frank admission from the beautiful actress. Why, she sounded almost friendly!

Seconds later, she felt a ripple of tension travel around the set. Without turning around, she knew Rex had just walked in. The hairs on the back of her neck rose fractionally as her body reacted automatically to his nearness. She had never been so vibrantly aware of any man as she was of him.

Watching Laine, she could see a similar reaction. The difference was, Rex returned Laine's love, Belle was convinced. Along with the others, she waited for the two to meet, although her anxiety was fuelled more by her feelings for Rex than curiosity.

Laine broke the silence first. 'Hello, Rex. I heard you were on the island and have been wondering where you were.'

He paused close to Belle, his breathing a light wind across her scantily clad shoulders. 'Hello, Laine. I'm surprised you even noticed I wasn't here.'

There was a perceptible indrawing of breath from the onlookers, Belle included. However, Laine chose to ignore the slight taunt. 'I always notice you, Rex, present or absent. What have you been doing with yourself? Oh, and how is your dear mother?'

It was said as the most innocent of enquiries but only Belle noticed the effect it had on Rex. He was standing at her shoulder and she saw him flinch as if stung. His eyes seemed to sink far back into his head and his bronzed skin assumed a greyish cast. Was she the only one seeing it? And why should such an innocent question have such a devastating effect?

'My mother is frail and ill,' he said carefully. 'I wouldn't like to see anything upset her.'

Laine inclined her head. 'Of course not. I understand the slightest upset could harm her.'

Belle remembered Rex saying how fragile his mother's health was. But this exchange seemed to hold more meaning than just a polite enquiry. What were Rex and Laine really saying to each other?

Laine was the first to break the spell. 'It's been nice seeing you again, Rex. Now I must go and wash this make-up off, then dive into the pool. I'm positively dripping.'

Rex nodded tautly and turned back the way he had come. The spell was broken for the rest of the crew, too. They had been standing like wax figures in a Tussaud tableau, watching the meeting. Now, they came back to life and went about their various tasks.

On impulse, Belle walked quickly after Rex. She caught up with him much further down the beach, where they were shielded from the others by a craggy outcrop of rock. 'What was that all about?' she asked, mystified.

He shrugged. 'What was what all about?'

'All that stuff about you and Laine and your mother?'

'Just what it sounded like.'

'The hell it was! You two were talking in some sort of code, as if she was giving you a warning and you were taking it.'

Rex whirled on her, fury darkening his craggy features. 'You should work for a scandal sheet with a mind like that! I already told you, it's none of your business.'

But I love you, that makes it my business, she cried inwardly, wishing she had the right to voice the words aloud. Instead, she said stiffly, 'All right, it is none of my business, but I want you to know I'm here if...if you ever need me.'

It sounded lame and foolish, but she was surprised to see the anger drain from his face. 'Thanks,' he said hoarsely. 'I only wish I could tell you the whole story, but I can't—for a lot of reasons, the main one being that I don't want to see you get hurt.'

So she was right. He was still in love with Laine, and he wanted to warn Belle before she became too attached to him. How else could she get hurt?

Unable to mask the misery in her eyes, she dropped her lashes over them. 'I understand,' she said softly.

His hand came under her chin, drawing her face up so she was forced to look at him. 'I wonder if you do.'

With a cry of dismay, she turned and fled back towards the house.

He watched her go with an ache in his heart. Damn Laine for showing up now, just when he had started to relax and enjoy Belle's company. Luckily, Laine didn't know how he felt about Belle. And he would make sure she didn't find out. Because if she did, Belle would see another side to the diminutive British actress.

So far, they had seen only the English Rose side, the one she had projected so winningly when Rex had first met her. It was only when he'd got to know her that he'd discovered the granite personality hidden under the fragile exterior.

Laine was a survivor and she didn't care at what cost. If she felt threatened by Belle, she wouldn't hesitate to attack, using any weapon at her disposal—and she had plenty. He, of all people, knew that. And both Belle and his mother would be the ones to suffer.

Why he cared so much about Belle, he still wasn't sure. She was a lovely girl—woman, he corrected inwardly. But it was more than her looks which appealed to him. Looks were a dime a dozen in Hollywood, and even more common on Australia's golden beaches.

Belle had something else, a candour about her which was rare and precious. Unlike Laine, Belle was prepared to stand or fall on her own merits. In fact, it was her drive to be judged on her merit alone, rather than her famous name, which he admired. Laine used every trick in the book to get where she wanted. Belle had thrown the book away long ago.

He shook his head in annoyance. Instead of cataloguing Belle's virtues, shouldn't he be trying to find fault with her? If he kept this up, he would head straight back to the villa and tell her how he really felt about her.

Then she would be well and truly at Laine's mercy.

Laine was reclining elegantly on a lounger beside the pool by the time Belle calmed herself enough to go back to the villa.

In a high-cut apricot *maillot*, Laine looked lithe and golden. She had removed her stage make-up and her English peaches-and-cream complexion glowed from the scrubbing. She hailed Belle warmly.

'Come and sit with me for a while, Belle. It's so nice to have a woman my own age to talk to, and we never get a moment to ourselves on the set.'

Belle's eyebrows tilted. Despite her fragile appearance, Laine was a good five years older than Belle, so the chumminess sounded forced. She made herself smile back, telling herself she was being unfair. Laine was hardly to blame because Belle had foolishly fallen for Rex.

'I hope you don't mind me making myself at home here,' Laine said when Belle sat down opposite her.

'Of course not. I'm glad you feel you can.'

Laine's green eyes roved over her surroundings approvingly. 'This is a glorious place. You're so lucky.'

Given that Laine was the one Rex cared for, Belle didn't feel lucky, but she inclined her head. 'My father had the foresight to buy the place before it became fashionable. I've been coming here since I was a child, so I sometimes take it for granted.'

'Then you're luckier than you know. I worked with your father in London once. He's a charming man.'

'Oh? What was the production?'

'It was the first Shakespearean season he did over there, but I only had a tiny walk-on part, so he wouldn't remember me.'

Belle shook her head. 'I wouldn't be too sure. Dad has an amazing memory.'

Laine's eyes shone. 'He was very kind, even to the minor players like me. It must be wonderful to have a father like that.'

Presuming she meant having a father in the same industry, Belle asked, 'Doesn't your family approve of your acting?'

Laine shrugged. 'Who knows? I was adopted as a baby, but my adopting mother died and her husband remarried. Once he discovered he could have children by his new wife, I became something of an inconvenience.'

'I'm sorry,' Belle said, at the same time wondering what had prompted the burst of confidences. She did feel sorry for the other woman, growing up feeling unwanted, but she still couldn't see why Laine was telling her about it.

She soon found out.

'It's all right, that's all behind me now,' Laine continued. 'Especially now that Rex and I have resolved our differences.'

Suddenly, Belle understood Rex's concern that she might get hurt. He had been trying to tell her that he and Laine were getting back together.

'Yes,' Laine went on dreamily, 'Coming here to see Rex has made all the difference. I don't feel so alone any more.'

It was out before Belle could prevent it. 'Then I'm surprised you left Rex in the first place, if you felt so strongly about him.'

Laine leaned forward confidentially. 'I didn't leave him. The break-up was a publicity stunt, to give my career a boost. When my agent suggested it, Rex was totally against the idea, but he soon saw how useful all those headlines would be for both of us.'

Belle felt ill. Why hadn't she thought of such a thing? In the film world, all sorts of crazy stunts took place in the name of publicity.

It explained so much: why Rex was so evasive about his break-up with Laine, and the 'coincidence' of his meeting here with the crew of Laine's film.

Belle had been little more than a pleasant diversion until the other woman arrived.

She rose, feeling numb, but was careful to mask her shock from Laine's searching gaze. The other woman touched her hand. 'I know this is a surprise to you, but please don't say anything to the rest of the crew. We want to wait until Rex's mother is better so we can include her in an announcement of our reunion.'

So that was what the veiled conversation was about on the set this morning! Once Laine knew Rex's mother was still in danger, she had to go on with the pretended estrangement from Rex. Why hadn't she seen all this before?

But it wasn't for Laine that she agreed to keep their secret. Enough of the crew had seen her mooning around Rex, so she would look a perfect fool if the truth came out now. 'I won't say anything,' she promised.

'Thanks. I knew I could count on you. Rex was right, you're a friend in need.'

Just what that need was, Laine couldn't begin to guess, Belle thought miserably. She felt a fraud, accepting Laine's compliments when all the while she was wishing the other woman to another planet.

'You won't let on to Rex that you know, will you?' Laine asked anxiously.

He would be the last person she would confide in, she thought furiously. He had used her, even letting her protect him from the Press, all the time knowing he was still in love with Laine. 'I won't say anything,' she vowed readily.

'Good. There's just one more thing.'

Drained of emotion, she regarded Laine incuriously. 'Yes?'

'I hope you don't think I'm being too presumptuous, but I'd like to give a party for the crew, here on the beach. I'd fly in all the food and drink from the mainland, so you wouldn't have to lift a finger. Please say you don't mind?'

A party was the last thing Belle felt like right now but she nodded mechanically. 'Of course not. Dad said you were to treat the place as your own.'

'Super! I take it you'll come, then?'

'I don't know. I'm not much of a partygoer,' Belle dissembled.

'But it's the wrap party to celebrate the end of location filming, and you're one of the stars. You simply must come.'

'I'll see,' Belle compromised.

At this, Laine settled back on her lounger, the conversation clearly over. But as an afterthought, she added, 'By the way, will you tell Rex about the party? He's definitely invited.'

Of course he was, Belle acknowledged inwardly. Her own invitation was a formality. It was Rex who Laine really wanted to invite. 'I'll pass on the message and he can give you his answer himself,' she said, tired of being their go-between.

Laine patted her hand in sisterly fashion. 'Thanks a lot. I'm glad we had this talk. I feel we understand each other so much better now.'

Oh yes, Belle thought as she made her way into the villa. She understood Laine perfectly.

CHAPTER SEVEN

AFTER her conversation with Laine, Belle was surprised when Rex asked her to accompany him to the wrap party.

'Won't you be going with Laine?' she asked, thinking aloud.

He gave an impatient sigh and his mouth settled into a harsh line. 'If I was, would I be asking you?'

Yes, she thought crossly. It would provoke less gossip if he was seen with Belle, keeping alive the myth that he and Laine were estranged.

All the same, she knew she would accept, because it might be her last chance to enjoy his company before the truth came out and he moved beyond her reach for good. It was crazy, but she found she wanted to spend that time with him. With this in mind, she dressed with special care that evening, even while acknowledging that Rex's eyes were unlikely to be on her.

Her choice was an exotic evening jumpsuit in fluid crêpe de Chine. The sensual fabric outlined every curve of her lithe body, and the exotic print in mauve and jade made her skin glow with youthful life.

Looking at the final effect in her mirror, she sighed. Was there anything more disheartening than gearing up for a battle one already knew to be lost?

Then she recalled her father's injunction when he had had to face a crowd of critics, after a harsh review early in his career. 'Never let 'em know they've got you licked,' was his sage advice and she decided to follow it now. The game might be over as far as Laine was concerned, but there was no need to give in *too* gracefully.

At seven-thirty, there was a knock on her door. 'Ready?' came Rex's softly voiced query.

She opened the door and her heart almost stopped at the sight of him framed in the opening. Black silk trousers clung to his long legs, emphasising every taut muscle, while his white mesh shirt teased her senses with a hide-and-seek effect of curling chest hairs glimpsed through the open weave. A rust-coloured sweater was knotted casually around his shoulders against the rapidly cooling evening.

For Belle, the effect was anything but cooling, and her pulses began to race. Each intake of breath filled her nostrils with the aroma of his aftershave lotion, a potent mix of wood and leather which planted unwanted ideas in her head.

'You look terrific,' she breathed, seconds after resolving not to comment at all.

He leaned indolently against her door-frame, his eyes working their way from the bandeau top of her jumpsuit with its revealing expanse of creamy

skin, to the slim fit of her evening trousers over
strappy sandals which were foolishly fine-heeled for
a beach party. 'So do you,' was all he said, but he
managed to convey a great deal more.

'You look sexy and exciting,' was what she read
into his comment, because the effect her appearance had on him was visible in his darkening
eyes.

She had to remind herself that she was nothing
more than a decoy tonight, keeping the place at his
side warm for Laine, who had made her real po-
sition perfectly clear.

To hide the pain this thought brought with it, she
swung around and picked up her evening bag. 'We
mustn't keep Laine waiting, must we?' she said
overbrightly.

He blinked quickly, as if dispelling fantasies of
his own. 'No, I guess we mustn't.'

As they emerged into the moonlight, Belle drew
an involuntary breath of admiration. Even though
she had seen this sight so many times before, it never
failed to stir her senses.

In the silver light, the sand glowed and the water
reflected the myriad-coloured lights the film crew
had strung between the trees fringing the beach.

True to her word, Laine had ordered all the food
and drink from the mainland. It had arrived in
huge, white styrofoam containers that morning.

Now, the crew's caterers were busy setting it out
on long trestle-tables placed on the sand. Surveying
the groaning plates of lobster, oysters, scallops,

prawns, whole suckling pig and salads, Belle had to agree that Laine did things in style.

Everyone was in high spirits, rejoicing in the happy thought that all the location scenes were safely 'in the can'.

Sammy Durant, drink in hand, sailed over to intercept them. 'How's my little jungle queen?'

'Tired, but happy,' she acknowledged. 'If I'd known how much fun your film would be, you wouldn't have had to talk me into making it.'

'All's well that ends well,' Sammy said. 'Can I get you a drink?'

'I'll take care of Belle, thanks, Sam,' Rex said smoothly. 'She's *my* jungle queen this evening, remember?'

He sounded so sincere that she felt a surge of anger. He was playing his part to the hilt, pretending that he had eyes for no one but Belle, in case anyone thought otherwise. She must be mad, letting him use her like this!

But Sammy didn't notice anything amiss. 'Of course, of course,' he said jovially. He waved to someone over Rex's shoulder and excused himself to greet the new arrival.

'Aren't you overdoing things a bit?' she asked Rex crossly when Sammy was out of earshot. 'Your jungle queen, indeed!'

Rex raised a quizzical eyebrow. 'Sorry. I didn't mean to sound possessive, if that's what's bothering you.'

'You know perfectly well what's bothering me,' she hissed back. 'You see, I know why you asked me to be your partner tonight.'

He had the grace to look discomfited. 'I hadn't realised my motives were so transparent.' Then he brightened. 'But you agreed to come, so you can't object too much.'

'Let's say I'm philosophical about it.'

Now he definitely looked interested. 'Are you now? Does that mean you might be seeing things my way for once?'

Good grief! What other way could she see them, when he had everything arranged so much to his advantage? This way, he could enjoy Laine's company at the party, and no doubt arrange something more private afterwards, while having the benefit of Belle's presence on his arm to allay suspicion.

What a fool she was, Belle told herself. She had thought it would make a difference, having Rex as her escort tonight. But it only served to remind her that she was the odd woman out. Whoever said it was better to have loved and lost was out of their minds. It was better not to have got into this mess at all!

She went through the motions of greeting the others, sipping champagne and nibbling canapés. All the time, she felt like an extra on a set, painfully aware that she was an actress playing the part of Rex's new love interest.

Laine was at her most dazzling tonight, shining in a silver sarong which skimmed her petite figure and left little to the imagination.

Belle was achingly aware of the way the other woman's eyes darted back to Rex, as if he was a kind of security blanket for her. It was as if she needed to know where he was at any given moment.

At last, the actress came over to them. 'Rex, darling! I'm so glad you could tear yourself away from your idyllic life-style to join the workers.'

Rex laughed hollowly. 'Some workers! Living it up on a tropical island. My heart bleeds for all of you.'

The sense of a secret shared between them was so powerful that it made Belle feel weak. Although they talked superficially, she was aware of an undercurrent between them, of things unspoken that only they knew about.

Seeing them together, knowing what they shared, she was finally forced to accept that the relationship was far from over. How could it be when every word Rex and Laine spoke carried a hidden message?

Belle looked around at the others. Couldn't they sense what was going on? Or was she the only one to recognise the bond between Rex and Laine? She shivered, feeling burdened by her knowledge.

There was a stirring at the poolside as more of the crew arrived, their identities veiled by the darkness. Laine touched Rex's arm. 'I'd better circulate. Catch up with you later.'

She didn't add 'darling' and yet she did. There was also a promise in her parting words. So Rex *did* intend to meet Laine later, under cover of darkness.

Suddenly, Belle became tired of the game. Being with Rex like this wasn't fun, nor was it anything she would care to remember later on. How could it be pleasant when he was mentally with another woman?

She stepped closer to him, conscious of how Laine's spicy perfume lingered in the air around him. 'I think I'll call it a night. I...I have a headache.'

He looked at her keenly. 'I would think a writer could be more original than that.'

'All right, so I don't have a headache. I've just had enough of all this.'

'I know what you mean. Show business parties are all the same, aren't they? So why don't we go off somewhere by ourselves, just you and me?'

Just you and me. How wonderful it sounded. A few days ago she would have been thrilled by such a suggestion. But tonight, knowing how little the invitation meant, she shook her head. 'It wouldn't be a good idea.'

She had no intention of getting in any deeper than she was already.

He accepted her refusal with good grace. 'All right, then I'll see you back inside. We can talk there, if you prefer.'

It wasn't what she wanted at all, but before she could press him to stay at the party and let her go in alone, she felt him stiffen beside her. 'What's the matter?'

'Damn,' he said under his breath. 'Somebody's invited that pesky journalist, Harry Crossinger.'

She followed his gaze to where Laine was welcoming some new arrivals. As they moved into the light, Belle recognised the journalist among them. 'I suppose being a film writer, he must know quite a few people here.'

'Like Laine for one,' was his angry response. 'She probably heard he'd been sniffing around and couldn't resist the chance of a few more headlines.'

Now that she knew what lengths the other woman would go to for publicity, Belle could easily accept this notion. 'What are you going to do?' she asked. 'We can't leave without going right past him.'

'You're right,' Rex agreed. He grasped her hand and led her quickly into the house. 'Do you have your make-up kit with you?'

'Yes, but I don't...' Understanding soon followed. 'Clark Rider!'

'Exactly.'

Ten minutes later, after they had crept back to the party, she left it conspicuously on the arm of her wimpy-looking boyfriend, 'Clark'. If anything, he looked even worse than the first time, with his hair slicked down and the glasses drooping over his nose. He had pulled up the legs of his trousers so they looked too short for him. 'How do I look?'

She suppressed a giggle. 'Terrible—Clark.'

He gave her a warning look, then took her arm and they continued their stroll across the beach, their goal being Belle's electric car.

Spotting Belle, Harry Crossinger stepped across their path. 'Good evening, Miss Fraser, and Mr Rider, wasn't it?'

'You have a good memory, Mr Crossinger,' she said sweetly. 'You remember Mr Crossinger from the *Enquirer*, don't you, Clark, darling?'

'Gee, I've met so many famous people since I came here, Belle. It's just wonderful. Nice to see you again, Mr Crossinger,' he simpered and held out a limp hand.

Distastefully, the journalist took it, then pulled free as quickly as he could and looked around. 'Your other house guest, Rex Marron, is joining us tonight, I understand.'

She clucked her tongue. 'Still looking for the phantom film star, Mr Crossinger! I told you, there's nobody here but Clark and me, and the film crew, of course.'

'My tip says he's here,' the journalist persisted.

'Well, in that case, good hunting,' she said and stepped adroitly around him. Before anyone else could accost them, she hurried 'Clark' across the remaining stretch of sand and slid into the driver's seat of her car. Rex leaned over her. 'Would you like me to drive?'

She shook her head. 'I know these roads. Now get in before anyone else spots us.'

He did as bidden and they were soon driving along the moonlit stretch of track which led out of the colony to the tourist areas on the other side of the island.

'The others will wonder where we got to,' she observed as she drove.

'No, they won't. They'll think we're enjoying a lovers' tryst in some dark corner of the colony. Hell—they will, won't they?'

Suddenly he realised the significance Laine would attach to his disappearance with Belle. Damn! He had been so busy protecting himself from the gutter press that he hadn't given a thought to how things would look for Belle. Well, there was nothing he could do about it now except hope that Laine wouldn't feel threatened if she found out, otherwise there would be hell to pay.

'Where would you like to go?' Belle asked in a taut voice. His sudden quietness when she had mentioned what the others would think told its own story. He was only now realising how it would look to Laine. He should have thought of that before he enlisted Belle's help to get him out of a spot.

'You sound angry,' he said out of the darkness. 'Are you sorry about missing the party?'

'I couldn't care less about the party,' she almost spat back.

'Then it must be your reputation you're concerned about. In which case, we'll go somewhere nice and public where there are lots of crowds to protect your honour.'

Which would suit him very well, Belle realised. Later, if Laine questioned his absence, he would have plenty of witnesses to allay her suspicions.

'How about the underwater observatory?' she suggested snidely. 'There are plenty of crowds there.'

To her surprise, he agreed readily. There were crowds all right, but of fish, not people. At this hour of the evening, near to closing time, they were the only human visitors.

However, the viewing windows were crowded with tiny fish, hanging motionless as they slept in their schools. Orange-striped soldier fish glinted as if floodlit, and the banks of coral shone phosphorescent in the spill of light from the observatory chamber.

It was a magical sight, enough to make Belle forget how annoyed she was with Rex. As she watched the night-feeding corals extend their polyps and bloom into colour, she relaxed a little. Why not take the evening at face value, and enjoy herself in his company? It would be easy to pretend they were really on a date, perhaps the first of many, leading to something more serious, and forget that anyone else existed.

'You've brightened up somewhat,' Rex noticed when they made their way back up the steel stairs and out into the star-bright night.

Since she didn't want to annoy him by sharing her game of let's pretend, she just smiled. 'It's a beautiful evening. I decided I might as well enjoy myself.' It was close enough to the truth to satisfy them both.

He linked an arm through hers. 'In that case, we'll stay here and have dinner at the Poisson d'Or, hopefully without any interruptions this time.' He chuckled softly. 'That is, if you don't mind spending the evening with a character like Clark Rider.'

She made her tone equally playful. 'Why not? He is the love of my life, isn't he?'

She only hoped he didn't guess how close to the truth it was.

If the restaurateur hadn't recognised Belle, they would have been refused a table, since the restaurant was crowded. Last time, Rex had been instantly recognised and the service had been impeccable.

This time, in his Clark Rider disguise, he went unrecognised and the attitude of the management was quite different.

'Maybe being famous isn't such a curse, after all,' Belle laughed. Not long ago he had been complaining about the zealous attention of the Press. Now he was complaining because he attracted no attention.

Rex sighed. 'I guess you're right. We all want what we can't have. When it comes within our reach, we find we don't want it as much as we thought we did.'

'Keep this up and I'll start believing there's a real philosopher underneath that Hollywood veneer,' Belle said. 'First you lecture me about letting go of the past, and now you're waxing lyrical about wanting being more desirable than having. You continually surprise me, Mr Marron.'

'Rider, please!' he said in mock alarm. Then his gaze softened. 'I like surprising you, Belle. It means you're intrigued, and I like that.'

She lowered her gaze. Knowing he wanted to intrigue her came as a surprise. She would have thought he would prefer to put as much emotional distance between them as he could.

Instead, he seemed to want to get to know her better. All through dinner he questioned her about her hopes and ambitions, and the way she felt about the world in general.

Coming from a man like Rex, the attention was flattering and dangerously heady. She had to constantly remind herself that he was not hers for the taking. His affections lay elsewhere and he was only making an effort to charm her tonight in return for rescuing him from the journalist.

All the same, she found herself succumbing and answered his most probing questions with frankness and a lack of guile that, had she but known it, entranced him.

He raised his champagne glass to her. 'A toast, to a most unusual lady,' he said softly.

Flustered, she lowered the glass she had automatically raised in response. 'I'm not unusual, Rex, honestly. I'm just your run-of-the-mill actress, a product of the dream factory. Don't make me into something I'm not, please.'

His eyes were grave as he sipped the champagne. 'I repeat the toast. You are an unusual lady, Belle. In a world of silver plate, you're sterling silver.'

Feeling the colour flood into her face, she pressed her fingers to his lips. 'Stop, you're embarrassing me.'

Before she could pull them back, his lips moulded themselves around her fingertips, imprisoning them in a kiss which was more sensuous than anything she had ever experienced.

She felt a stirring of response deep within her and looked at him with wide, sensation-drugged eyes as she slowly lowered her hand. 'Oh, Rex, why do you keep doing this to me?'

'Because you keep doing it to me,' was his laboured response. He signalled for their bill. 'Let's get out of here. Suddenly it's much too crowded.'

She felt a shiver of desire ripple through her from head to toe. Every instinct told her she should get into her car and head back to the villa right now, before...

Before what? The look in Rex's eyes promised the world, and tonight, she knew she wanted it. She wasn't running away, not this time.

By the time they had paid their bill and emerged into the night air which was freshened by a light breeze from the sea, she was almost giddy with the certainty of what she was going to do.

If Rex wanted her, she was his. Never mind whether it was for a minute, an hour or a day. It would be enough. In that one, sweet moment she knew the meaning of the phrase, ''tis better to have loved and lost, than never to have loved at all'.

If she never gave herself the chance to love Rex Marron because she knew she must lose him, she would regret it for the rest of her life.

'You're very quiet,' he observed as they strolled along the promenade edging the beach. 'What are you thinking?'

'Romantic thoughts,' she said truthfully.

Under the shadow of a swaying palm tree, he stopped and turned her to face him. 'That's funny, so was I.'

She could hardly breathe for wanting him. 'Of me?'

'Of you, my beautiful Belle.'

'Oh, Rex!'

When he increased the pressure on her arms to draw her against him, she offered no resistance, melting into his embrace as if she belonged there. It was like a homecoming.

But the best was still to come when he bent his head and sought her willing mouth. He had kissed her before, but never with such passion. It was as if he was igniting fires deep within her. The flames, fanned by the pressure of his mouth against hers, danced higher and higher until she felt they must consume both of them.

Laine Grosvenor might not have existed. There was only Belle Fraser and the man she loved. She wished that this moment would never end.

All her doubts and fears were swept away in an aching, throbbing awareness of her need of him. One more second and she knew she would be his, whatever the consequences.

Suddenly, she felt him tense in her arms and he slid away from her, turning to lean against the railing facing out to sea. It was too swift. She felt deserted. Then she knew the reason for his sudden change of heart.

'There you are, Rex. I do hope I'm not late.'

If Rex had struck her, Belle couldn't have felt the betrayal more keenly. Tears of annoyance and disappointment crowded her eyes and she brushed at them angrily. All this was a set-up, and she had fallen for it like a complete innocent.

'So you had to get away from the journalist, did you?' she said to Rex's back. 'What a pity you didn't tell me what you were escaping to.'

'Belle, please let me explain,' he appealed, turning towards her.

She silenced him with a gesture. 'Laine's waiting for you. What else is there to explain?'

'Look, I didn't know she was coming here tonight.'

'Like you didn't know she was coming to the island?' she said bitterly. 'I'm sorry, Rex, I just don't like being used. I thought it would be a fair price for being with you tonight, but the price is just too high. I'm sorry.'

She left him standing in the shadows and stalked past Laine, who watched her go with a smile of satisfaction on her face.

Belle didn't look back. She didn't want to see them together, even though she knew they belonged that way. She was the interloper, not Laine. She had known it all along, even while she was trying to pretend things were different.

She had believed what she wanted to believe and she had no one to blame but herself if she got hurt. That's what usually came of playing with fire.

Oblivious to everything but her own inner pain, she was almost blinded by twin beams of light cutting across her path. They came from the water and she heard the throb of powerful engines as a boat approached the jetty alongside her.

Moments later a voice reached her out of the darkness. 'Ahoy there, is that you, Belle Fraser?'

She peered into the light and could make out three figures aboard the cruiser. One of them she recognised. 'Frank Bright, is it you?'

'It's himself, himself,' came a patently faked Irish accent. 'Will ye be comin' aboard, colleen?'

He sounded so cheerful that she smiled through her tears, but shook her head. 'No, thank you, I'm driving back to the villa.'

'Aw, come aboard and have a spin with us,' Frank implored. 'You missed a hell of a good party. You can't turn down our shindig as well.'

From the sound of him, he had already started on his 'shindig' and she didn't think it would be wise to go aboard the boat, even though in close-up she recognised the other two passengers as members of the film crew.

She was about to frame a stronger refusal when she heard footsteps hurrying up the promenade. 'Belle, wait—we have to talk.'

She couldn't stand any more of his evasions to-night. On impulse, she grasped Frank's out-stretched hand and jumped aboard the cruiser. 'All right, anchors aweigh,' she said, trying to sound light-hearted, while wishing desperately that Frank would stop fumbling with the mooring rope and pull away from the jetty before Rex reached the end of it.

When he saw they were about to cast off, his steps quickened. 'Belle, wait!'

Frank looked at her questioningly. 'Shall we wait for Rex?'

'No, he's driving my car back. Let's just get going,' she urged.

With a shrug, he freed the stubborn rope and signalled to the other man, who opened the throttle. The boat, which had been idling at the jetty, roared into life and they were soon some distance from the shore.

Looking back, she could see Rex silhouetted against the sky, a dark, solitary figure. Her heart turned over and she almost told Frank to go back, then Laine's petite figure appeared behind him. She hardened her heart. He had shown her where his loyalties lay. They had no more to talk about.

CHAPTER EIGHT

Resolutely, she turned away from the shore and smiled a greeting at the other two passengers.

'You know Maureen and Ken from the crew,' Frank offered.

'Oh yes, you're in Make-up,' she placed Maureen.

'And I'm Frank's Focus Puller,' Ken explained.

They were a nice enough crowd, although they all seemed the worse for champagne, probably the dual effects of Laine's party and the drinks they were handing around now, Belle thought a little anxiously.

She shook her head when Frank held out a glass for her. 'No thanks, Rex and I had wine with dinner.'

Frank shrugged and refilled the glass for himself. 'So that's where you two disappeared to. Laine was asking after you both.'

'That's putting it mildly,' Maureen giggled. 'She was spitting chips, especially when Sammy said he thought he'd seen you two drive off across the island.'

Belle frowned. Had Laine followed them of her own accord? She'd been so sure Rex had arranged the rendezvous that she hadn't allowed for this possibility, and it made her so uncomfortable that she dismissed it instantly. 'I'm sorry we had to leave the party,' she told Maureen, 'but a journalist turned up that Rex has been dodging all week.'

'You mean Harry Crossinger from the *Enquirer*?' Ken contributed. 'You needn't have worried. He didn't stick around once it was obvious that Rex wasn't going to show. He's going back to the mainland tomorrow, then heading south to cover the lead-up to the Logie Awards. He said this was his last chance to finish his inside story on Rex and Laine.'

'Laine was willing enough,' Maureen added. 'The clincher was to be a photo of Rex and Laine together. It would have been the first one taken since they broke up and would have been worth a fortune to the press.'

So Rex was right. Laine was headline-grabbing, Belle mused. Well, at least Rex could relax now that the journalist was leaving the island.

The boat aquaplaned off a large wave and a jet of spray hit Belle in the face, bringing her to her senses abruptly. What on earth were they doing out here, so far from shore?

'Shouldn't we be heading around to the lee of the island?' she asked nervously. 'These waters are treacherous enough by day. In the dark, we could easily run aground on the Reef.'

Frank laughed at her discomfort. 'Relax, honey, Ken here was technical advisor on Jacques Cousteau's last documentary.' He hesitated. 'Or was it

Ben Cropp's? It doesn't matter, because he knows these reefs like the back of his hand. Don't you, Ken?'

From the flying bridge, Ken looked down at her and saluted. 'Sure I do. I grew up in Townsville.'

All the same, she wasn't reassured. Even Captain Cook had run aground in these waters when he first discovered Australia. And Ken was no Captain Cook.

'I still think we should head back to Main Bay,' she said firmly. The Reef waters were beautiful, silvered by moonlight as they were now, but they were still among the world's most dangerous.

The magnificent colour changes from delicate blue to deepest green, which were so admired by visitors, were created where the coral banks and ramparts were separated by tortuous channels. By night there was little to distinguish the channels.

'Relax, and have some champagne,' Frank urged.

She shook her head. 'Where are you heading?'

Ken answered from the bridge. 'Maureen has a yen to go snorkelling. We were talking about it at the party and it seemed like a good idea.'

She drew a sharp breath. 'Snorkelling at night? You're all crazy! The sharks will have you for a midnight snack.'

The genuine terror in her voice communicated itself at last to Frank. 'You really are scared out here, aren't you?'

'Yes, I am.' For good measure, she added, 'Also I'm not...not a very good sailor. I don't feel at

all well. I should have warned you.' The very real
fear she felt for their safety leant a convincing
tremor to her voice.

'We'll have to turn back, Belle's ill,' Frank told
Ken.

There was a sigh of disappointment from the
others. 'No moonlight swim? Aw, gee...'

Belle could only feel tremendous relief that they
had bought her seasick act. In truth, she was a fantastic sailor and had often accompanied her father
on sailing holidays up and down the Whitsunday
Passage. But it was all she could think of to make
Frank and his party return to the safety of the
beach. She dreaded to think what could happen to
them if they went diving on the Reef by night, especially after they'd been drinking.

She turned a shaky face to Frank. 'I will have
that drink now, please.'

She sipped it slowly, only starting to relax when
the shadowy bulk of Mana Island came back into
view. It rose high out of the water, a dark mass of
volcanic rock and coral. The sides were clothed in
grasslands and rain forest and looked black and
forbidding by night, in contrast to the sparkling
whiteness of the surf beaches fringing the shores.
Belle had never been so glad to see the island on
the horizon as she was now.

But instead of returning to the public jetty at
Main Bay, Ken steered the cruiser around the
coastline to a secluded beach which was locally
popular with nude sunbathers.

'Why are we pulling in here?' she asked.

Ken turned around and winked as he throttled back the powerful engine. 'Well, you see, I...er...borrowed this here boat.'

'You stole it?' she asked, horrified.

'No, I *borrowed* it. We have every intention of returning it to your neighbours when we've finished our midnight jaunt.'

'Now you wouldn't want us to wake them up at some unearthly hour just to ask to borrow their boat, would you?' Frank said reasonably.

She wondered what the Morrisons, who lived next door to the Frasers, would think of his rational argument. Somehow, she doubted whether Bill Morrison would be impressed. He was a very possession-conscious man and was always working on his boat. 'I think you'd better take the boat back right away,' she said in a low voice.

'All right, all right, no need to upset yourself,' Frank placated her. 'We'll just pull in at that little cove, Ken.'

Ken did as bidden, steering the boat with commendable skill through the narrow mouth of the cove and beaching it gently on a stretch of pristine white sand.

'There, I told you I was perfectly all right,' he said, then belied his words by stumbling as he climbed down from the flying bridge.

Belle offered up a silent prayer of thanks that they had made it back to the beach safely. Bill Morrison would have to collect his boat from the cove in the morning, because these three weren't putting out to sea again if she could help it.

In the end, she was unable to change their minds. They were deaf to all her arguments about the wisdom of cruising the Reef at night, and she was very much in the minority.

Frank patted her shoulder. 'Now you just settle yourself down here till you feel better. We'll be back for you in an hour and we'll all go safely home to bed. All right?'

'No, it isn't all right!' she spluttered. 'In the first place, I don't want to be stranded here, and in the second you're all going to get yourselves killed.'

'Don't worry about us,' Frank chuckled. 'Ken and I have been leading charmed lives for two decades. We're favourites of the gods, aren't we, Maureen?'

'Sure thing,' Maureen giggled. She was somewhat champagne-affected and not likely to be much help to Belle in changing Frank's mind.

But short of physically preventing them from leaving, there was nothing Belle could do except watch them push the boat out into deeper water. Despair assailed her as she heard the engine start its throaty growling again, then escalate into a high-pitched noise as they picked up speed.

In the still night air, she heard the engine for a long time, interspersed with laughter from the revellers, then it died away and she was alone on the beach.

Being left on the beach didn't frighten her. She had often camped out on different parts of the island as a child and she knew every beach and cove intimately. She was more frightened for the others.

They had promised to return in an hour, so she settled herself on the sand with her back against a pandanus palm, to wait for them.

She could only hope that Frank's gods were indeed looking after his favourites tonight, because they were going to need every ounce of luck to survive their insane plans.

Cursing the serendipity of all film people, she closed her eyes and let her thoughts wander with the gentle sea breezes.

Try as she might, they came back again and again to one person—Rex Marron. What was he doing now? Had he waited for her on the jetty, or was he already back at the colony with his precious Laine?

Probably the latter, she thought miserably, although she had only herself to blame. She had done nothing but rebuff him since he'd arrived. She must have been crazy to think she could redress all that with the promise of a night of love.

Thinking of his rejection brought a wave of pain with it. Maybe that was his way of getting even with her for playing games before. But she had been perfectly sincere tonight. She had wanted him to make love to her. Now, she didn't even have the consolation of having loved before she had lost him.

In her well of sand, still warm from the day's sun, with her back cradled against the tree, she began to fade. Her eyelids felt heavy and her whole body became a weight, sinking into the warm sand.

She was drifting. Drifting. The whispering breezes in the pandanus palms lulled her, as did the shushing of the waves against the sand. She slept.

It was only when the early-morning chill began to seep into her bones that she awoke with a start. She was shivering with cold, and her clothes were damp with dew.

Good lord! Her watch had stopped at two in the morning. Heaven only knew what time it was now or how long she had slept. The others should have returned for her ages ago.

Unless...her heart lurched and a sick feeling washed over her. Unless they'd had an accident and were never coming back at all. If only she had been able to persuade them not to put out to sea again!

She stood up, stumbling as her cramped legs protested. She stamped her feet to dispel the pins and needles, and wrapped her arms around herself to try to get warm.

This was useless. She would be better off walking back to the colony where she could summon help to organise an air-and-sea search of the area.

After a moment's hesitation, she decided to go back through the rain forest, following a track she'd taken hundreds of times before. It was the first time she'd tried it in darkness, but it was the fastest way back.

It would have been easier to follow the beach around, but now, at high tide, she would have had to clamber over treacherous rocks, possibly sustaining some coral cuts which healed slowly and painfully.

As she turned towards them, the jungle-covered hills looked forbidding, full of dark shadowy places and alive with the flap-flap of wings. They were only birds, she told herself firmly to silence the butterflies starting up in her stomach. She told herself this was only a scene from the film. She was Lara, the jungle queen, and this was her domain.

By pretending that the tangle of she-oaks, pandanus, poincianas and banyans was a movie set, she was able to plough ahead with increasing confidence.

By day, the dark greenery would be enlived by showers of brilliantly coloured tropical flowers. Now, there was only green-black profusion and the sound of little mountain streams in her ears.

Skirting the edge of a saltwater lagoon which was a haven for native birds, she stumbled on a tangle of vines and almost sprawled all her length.

'Lara, queen of the jungle, has eyes like a cat and is just as sure-footed,' she recited to herself as she regained her feet. 'Lara, queen of the jungle, is afraid of nothing.'

'Lara, queen of the jungle is a terrible liar,' she added, fighting the urge to giggle hysterically. Only the thought that the others might be depending on her to fetch help kept her going. That they might already be beyond help, she refused to consider.

When the ground became boggy beneath her feet, she knew she had reached the mangroves beyond which was the Fraser villa. She avoided the tangled roots by making a wide detour along the beach, emerging at the spot where Laine had held her beach party earlier. The sand was still littered with debris and light flickered from the coloured globes festooning the trees.

To Belle's surprise, the villa wasn't in darkness as she'd expected. Instead, it was ablaze with light, and there were lights on in many of the guest rooms flanking the pool.

She screamed as she stumbled against a bulky masculine body. A torch shone into her eyes, momentarily blinding her, and there was a muffled curse. 'Thank God, it *is* you, Belle!'

She collapsed against his familiar bulk. 'Sammy, thank goodness it's you!'

He put a steadying arm around her shoulders and supported her as they walked back towards the house. 'Hey, everybody, it's Belle, she's OK!' he called out in his booming voice which had brought many a movie set to a standstill.

'What do you mean? Of course I'm OK,' she said, puzzled.

'We thought you'd drowned,' he explained, his voice choked.

'Drowned? I don't understand.'

'Never mind now. You're safe, and that's all that matters. I wasn't looking forward to facing Mitch with the news that you'd . . . oh hell, I'm getting all emotional. Come inside and we'll talk.'

In perplexed silence, she let him escort her into the villa where a circle of anxious faces greeted her. There was no sign of Laine, but Rex was there and he looked furiously angry.

'Where the hell have you been?' he demanded and the others looked at him, shocked.

'Give the girl a minute,' Sammy said, defending her. He put a glass of something into her hand. She sipped it and found it was brandy. The warmth flowed through her.

'I'm all right, Sammy,' she assured him. 'But I'd like to know what all this is about.'

'Weren't you with Frank and the others on the cruiser?' Rex demanded.

'I was for a short while but when I found out they'd been drinking, I persuaded them to put me ashore. I tried to get them to stay with me, but they were determined to go out on the Reef.' She clutched a hand to her mouth. 'Oh God, they're not . . .'

Rex confronted her grimly. 'No, they're not. But it was a near thing. They turned the boat over on a coral bank just outside Main Harbour. If a marlin boat hadn't been heading off for an early start and seen the accident, they'd all have died out there.'

She felt the colour drain from her face. 'I should have talked them into staying.'

'It wasn't your fault. They're big boys, and mighty lucky ones,' Sammy assured her. 'As it is, they'll have to pay the cost of the cruiser they wrecked, which should teach them a lesson.'

Frank's gods must have been with them after all. 'Are they all right?'

'They sustained various injuries and they've been taken to the mainland for treatment, but they should be all right.' He turned to the others. 'We'd better cancel the search and get some rest.'

When Sammy and the others had filed out, leaving her alone with Rex, she said, 'What search?'

'When there was no sign of you, we thought you'd drowned in the accident. An air search was to get under way at daybreak.' Suddenly all the anger left his face. 'Oh God, Belle! I thought I'd lost you tonight.'

She was alarmed by the depth of despair in his voice. 'It's all right, I'm safe.'

He shook his head. 'No, it isn't all right. You ran off because you believed I'd used you as a cover in order to meet Laine tonight.'

'Well, didn't you?' she asked in a low voice. His concern was merely guilt because he thought he was to blame for her near-miss.

'No, I didn't.' His eyes searched her face, warming even as he looked at her. 'How can I make you believe me?'

'Does it matter what I think?'

He took the glass from her and crushed her to him so she could feel the frantic pounding of his heart through her clothes. 'It matters, because I want to marry you, Belle. Tonight, when I thought I'd lost you, I realised how much you mean to me. I want to marry you, my love.'

She felt light-headed, not sure she was hearing him aright. She placed both hands on his chest, putting a few needed inches of space between them. 'Wait, Rex. Are you sure this isn't just the worry talking?'

'Of course, but it's also the truth. When I thought you were lost on the Reef, I found I didn't want to go on. That's how much you mean to me, love.'

Weakly, she leaned against him, feeling the warmth of his hands across her back. 'But what about Laine? She told me your separation was a publicity stunt and that you were waiting for the right time to announce a reconciliation.'

He swore softly under his breath. 'So *that's* where you got the idea I was meeting her secretly.'

Hope welled in her like a rising flame. 'You mean, it isn't true?'

'No, it isn't.'

'But why would she make up something like that?'

'To keep you and me apart, which is exactly what she's managed to do.'

For a moment, Belle thought she must still be wandering in the rain forest and imagining all this. 'I don't understand any of this,' she said wearily.

He stroked the hair back from her forehead with a gentleness which brought tears to her eyes. 'It is a lot to take in, I know, especially after the night you've had. But just understand one thing, my darling. I love you and I want to marry you. Nothing else matters.'

Something was happening to her brain. Swirling clouds of mist kept gathering before her eyes, affecting her ability to think straight. She struggled to think through the haze. 'But Laine said . . .'

'I know, and it's time you knew the whole story before you give me the answer I pray you will give me. Are you up to hearing it now?'

'Of course I am,' she said impatiently, just seconds before the fog swirled all around her and she saw the floor rushing up to meet her.

CHAPTER NINE

REX'S anxious face swam into focus above her and she struggled to focus on him. He cradled her as she sat up, and continued to hold her. 'I'm sorry, I don't know what came over me,' she apologised.

He massaged her back and shoulders until she could feel the tension ebbing out of them. 'Don't apologise. I should have realised you needed more time to get over your ordeal out there. Would you like me to call a doctor?'

'No, I'm fine, really,' she insisted. 'I feel such a fool.'

'No more than I feel,' he said ruefully. 'Letting you take off in a boat with those idiots, and all because you misjudged my relationship with Laine.'

She fought down the hope which began to take root at his words. 'You'd better tell me what's going on here.'

He regarded her with soft-eyed concern. 'Are you sure you're up to it tonight? Maybe after a good night's sleep...'

'I shan't sleep a wink until I know the truth,' she said impatiently. 'Really, I'm fine now.'

All the same, he insisted she take a hot shower and change her clothes, then he fetched her another brandy and watched her until she had sipped at least half of it. Its warmth spread along her veins like fingers of fire. Then she set the glass down and crossed her arms, regarding him steadily. 'Well?'

He raked a hand through his dark hair, rumpling it. Then he fixed her with a steady gaze. 'First, I need to be sure that you feel the same way about me, Belle.'

Wearily, she shook her head. 'I'm not sure that I do. I know I love you, but I want something more lasting from love than I think you do.'

'Even though I told you I want to marry you?'

'I feel as if I pressured you into a proposal. After all, when you came here, you made it clear all you wanted was a holiday romance.'

He smiled nostalgically. 'So I did, when I arrived. I had been hurt and was feeling disillusioned about women. When I found we'd be sharing the villa, I felt we could dispense with the preliminaries. I really thought an affair with you would be enough to satisfy me.'

She could hardly speak for the lump in her throat. 'And wasn't it?'

'No. The better I came to know you, the more I realised I need you in my life, for good.'

To avoid meeting his eyes, she picked up her brandy and cradled the glass in front of her, the gesture instinctively protective. Swirling the liquid around in the glass, she stared into the amber depths. 'You know I feel the same way about you,' she confirmed. 'But I'm still confused about you and Laine.'

He lowered his head. 'There's no need. Hell, you have a right to know. Laine Grosvenor is my sister.'

She felt as if he had felled her with a blow. 'But the publicity... she was living with you...'

'She was living in my house, certainly. But we were never lovers. The papers made that up and I couldn't correct it without revealing the truth about our relationship.'

'But your sister,' Belle breathed, her thoughts whirling. 'How could that be? Laine is English.'

'So is my mother. Early in her career, she fell in love with an English actor. He deserted her when she found out she was pregnant. She had no security to offer the child and no choice but to have it adopted. After she became successful, she tried to trace the child, but failed.'

'Laine is that child,' Belle said flatly.

'Yes. She came here from England with papers which proved her identity and of course, my mother took her in straight away.'

Suddenly it was all clear to Belle. 'That's why you gave her a home and helped her to get started in films here.'

He nodded, his gaze hardening. 'I thought she was just a struggling young actress that Mum had befriended. You see, my mother was too ashamed of her past even to tell me about Laine. It came as quite a shock when Laine herself confronted me with the news that she was my half-sister.'

'But I still don't understand why you had to keep it a secret, knowing what the press would think of her living with you.'

'That didn't matter a damn. What worried me more was how my mother would react if the news became public. She's frail enough without being the centre of a scandal.'

'But surely it's all in the past now,' Belle ventured.

'A star's life is never in the past,' Rex said bitterly. 'Look how they still attack poor Marilyn Monroe, after all these years. And as Lenore Gale, my mother was a star in England.'

Belle touched his hand, the light gesture a bond between them. 'I see. So you let the media attack you instead.'

'It wasn't all that noble,' he insisted, colouring slightly. 'My mother did save my life in that plane crash. The least I can do is let her live out her last years in peace and dignity.'

One thing was still puzzling Belle. 'You said you were afraid the news would harm your mother if it got out. How could it if you three were the only ones who knew the truth?'

'Laine threatened to make her story public unless I got her bigger and bigger parts. When success didn't come as quickly as she wanted, she tried to use her charms on me to make me do her bidding.'

Shocked, Belle stared at him, her eyes wide. 'She did that knowing you were brother and sister?'

'There isn't much she won't stoop to if it will further her career,' he said grimly. 'I think she sensed she'd gone too far that time and volunteered to move out if I'd foot the bills for her.'

'And that's where the press got their "palimony" story from,' Belle concluded. 'Oh, Rex, how terrible for you.'

'There was nothing I could do about it without hurting my mother.' His shoulders slumped and the sea-green eyes darkened with pain. 'Now you see why I didn't want to involve you in this, knowing that Laine would stop at nothing to get what she wants.'

Her heart went out to him, even though there was nothing she could say to ease his pain. 'Surely Laine wouldn't stand in the way of your happiness.'

'She would if it threatened her future security,' he averred. 'As long as she has the power to destroy my mother, I can't take any risks with her.'

A tight knot of unhappiness formed in Belle's chest and she swallowed hard, seeking the strength to say the words she knew she must. 'Then there can be no future for us as long as your mother is vulnerable to Laine's threats.'

His eyes were full of regret as he faced her. 'I'm afraid so, my darling. I want to put my ring on your finger and tell the world that we belong to each other, but the risk is too great, to you as well as my mother.'

'There is another way,' she said softly, wondering at her own temerity. 'We could still belong together, as long as we are the only ones who know it.'

He touched her chin so her face came up and she met his searching look proudly. 'You would do that for me, even though I can't offer you a public commitment for God knows how long?'

She laughed softly, seductively. 'You flatter yourself, Mr Marron. I'd be doing it for me, too. If I can't have everything I want, I'm adult enough to settle for what I can have.'

'Oh, Belle.'

He reached for her and she swayed against him as his arms tightened around her. 'I love you, Rex,' she whispered into his shoulder, while his hand caressed her hair over and over.

With a groan of capitulation, he swept her up into his strong arms, the muscles of his many workouts more than a match for her slight weight. She leaned into the embrace and clasped her hands around his neck as he carried her to his room.

She thought he would carry her to the bed, but instead he set her down just inside the door. There, he gathered her into his arms so their bodies melded into one line.

When he kissed her, his mouth was fiery and demanding. Her lips, already molten, shaped themselves to his command.

A gasp of pure pleasure escaped her as he slid a hand in between the buttons of her shirt and found her breasts. Through her bra, she could feel the warmth of his touch as it became more and more urgent.

Her whole body vibrated with need of him until she felt as if she would explode at any moment.

As he sensed her surrender, his caresses became more intimate until, with an impatient gesture, he swept aside her shirt and reached for the fastening of her bra.

In the next instant, she stood before him, her golden skin glowing as she swayed towards him.

'Are you sure?' he ground out. 'There's still time to change your mind.'

As if she could, when every inch of her was trembling with anticipation. He had aroused her to such a pitch of feverish excitement that she could no more walk away now than she could fly.

'Yes, my darling,' was all she could say through constricted throat muscles.

It was enough.

He led her to the bed and drew back the covers, his eyes locked with hers. She reached for the fastening of her jeans, but he stayed her hand. 'Please, let me.'

Mesmerised by the warmth of his gaze, she allowed him to guide her on to the bed and lay quiescent while he unzipped her jeans and slid them slowly down the length of her legs. As his fingers trailed along her thighs, she arched her back, feeling wave after wave of desire wash over her.

He dealt with his own clothes more speedily, letting them drop where they would, until he was clad only in sleek black briefs which skimmed his lean hips. Then he shed those too, leaving her in no doubt as to his state of arousal.

When he lay beside her on the bed, the contact jolted her like an electric shock, and she almost pulled away from him. But he held her until the shock subsided and she curved willingly into his arms again.

With insistent, mind-shattering pressure, he massaged her breasts in turn into pert, expectant life. Her breathing quickened and her pulses fluttered at throat and wrist like captive birds.

'I love you, Belle,' he murmured, his mouth roving over hers, seeking and receiving a response she was powerless to withhold.

'I love you too,' she answered unhesitatingly. 'I think I've loved you since we first met.'

'All that time wasted,' he said in self-disgust.

'We aren't wasting it now,' she reminded him.

He kissed her again, long and deeply, putting into the embrace all the love he held for her. To realise how thoroughly she was loved took her breath away.

When he covered her body with his she was prepared, but still gasped with surprised delight when he claimed her. She had dreamed it would be like this, but this was real and every powerful thrust of his body emphasised it.

Together, they soared inexorably upwards to heights of pleasure they had never known before.

A new world of sensation opened before her and she explored it eagerly, her body acting almost of its own volition.

Just when it seemed as if there were no new heights to be scaled, they reached one more, the highest of all. There, they crested the peak together, then glided down the other side in shared ecstasy.

'My Belle, my wife,' he whispered as their breathing slowed at last.

'Yes, Rex. Even if no one in the world knows it but us.' She was his, in every way that mattered. What did it matter if there was no ring, no symbol, maybe not for a long time?

All the same, a small voice inside nagged that perhaps it did matter, just a little. What right had Laine to come between them like this, and all in the name of her ambition?

'Are you sure you don't mind?' he asked her as he cradled her in the darkness.

'Of course not. As long as I know you love me, it doesn't matter who else knows it,' she vowed. If only he knew how much she wanted to believe it herself.

She awoke to the pressure of an arm across her body, its weight warm and somehow welcoming. As she came fully awake, the memory of last night came flooding back and she turned her head. When her eyes met Rex's, he smiled languidly. 'Good morning, love.'

'I thought for a minute, I'd dreamed... everything,' she said with unaccustomed shyness.

'If you did, we shared the same dream. No regrets?'

Resolutely she shook her head. 'Not a one.'

His eyes brightened and he reached for her. 'Care to prove it?'

'Oh, Rex! What about the others?'

They both knew she meant Laine. 'They're packing, ready for the trip back to the mainland,' he explained. 'Soon we'll have the island all to ourselves again.'

It was a heady thought and her body trembled with the prospect of the days ahead of them. He felt the tremor and gathered her close against him. 'Not scared?'

'Of you? Never.' But maybe a little at what she had got herself into, she acknowledged. In giving herself to Rex, she'd made a pledge as binding as any marriage vow. Even though he could offer no more than a secret love for now, she had accepted it whole-heartedly.

Some day, when Rex had found a way to nullify Laine's threat, they would be together publicly. Until then, it was enough to know that Rex loved her.

Rex teased the frown from her forehead with a stroking finger. 'Such deep thoughts. Like to share them with me?'

She kissed the tip of his finger as it slid past her mouth. 'I want to share everything with you.'

He grinned. 'I thought we already did.'

'I was referring to my innermost thoughts,' she said primly, making him laugh again. The sound of it sent answering ripples of joy flooding through her. If only they could remain here in their cocoon of loving warmth, sharing laughter and secrets for ever...

The thought was shattered by a rap on the door. 'Rex, are you awake?'

At the sound of Laine's voice, Belle shot Rex a worried glance. When she gestured towards the open bathroom door, he nodded and she slipped out of bed, reaching for her clothes, which were scattered on the floor.

Carrying them, she slipped into the bathroom and pulled the door closed. As she dressed quietly, she wondered what Laine wanted so urgently.

Laine's voice projected clearly through the thin door, drawing Belle's attention reluctantly.

'I didn't want to disturb you before this, Rex, since there was nothing you could do, anyway.'

'Nothing I could do about what? Come on, Laine, what is it?'

'It's your mother.'

Rex drew an audible breath. 'Oh God, she's not...'

'No! It's all right,' came Laine's quick denial. 'But there was a phone call from the mainland this morning to say she's had some sort of relapse and she's asking for you.'

Belle could imagine Rex shaking Laine. 'For God's sake, woman, why didn't you call me to the phone?'

'It was only a message, and I knew you couldn't leave until the crew 'copter goes at lunch time, so what was the point?'

'You are the most unfeeling. . .' He broke off, his voice hoarse with emotion. 'Next time, I'll take my own messages and make up my own mind if they're important or not. Do you understand?'

'I'm sorry, Rex. The phone woke me from sleep and I suppose I wasn't thinking properly, otherwise I would have called you.'

She sounded so genuinely contrite that Belle wasn't surprised when she heard Rex's voice soften. 'It's all right, Laine. I'm sorry I took it the wrong way. Who called and what exactly did they say?'

Laine repeated the message carefully. It seemed that Lenore Marron's companion had called, giving the information that Mrs Marron had taken a turn for the worse and was asking for her son.

'What time was this?' Rex demanded. Belle wondered if he was thinking about the reason why he had been too preoccupied to hear the phone ringing.

'About four this morning. As I said, I wasn't too bright myself, after the excitement of the search last night.'

'I know, we all got to bed late,' Rex said flatly. 'God, how am I going to get to the mainland from here, in a hurry?'

There was a pause. 'There's nothing leaving the island till tomorrow. But the film company has charted a special 'copter to fly the crew back. There's one spare seat aboard. You could take it. There isn't much luggage space, but you could put some of what you'll need in my case and have the rest of your things sent on later.'

'All right. What time does the flight leave?'

'Around lunch time. Would you like the caterer to make you some food first, since you've missed breakfast?'

'No thanks. I don't feel like eating right now. I'd better start packing.'

Belle heard the bedroom door open. 'All right, Rex. I'll leave my suitcase open on my bed. Just put whatever you want into it and lock it up.'

'Thanks, Laine. I appreciate your help.'

There was the sound of the bedroom door closing and Belle heard the other woman's footsteps tap-tapping down the hall. Cautiously, she peered around the bathroom door. Rex was sitting dejectedly on the end of the bed.

She knelt beside him. 'I heard everything and I'm sorry, Rex. But you'll be home in a few hours. Everything will be all right.'

He gave her a wan smile. 'I guess so. I didn't want to leave my mother at all. I was afraid something like this would happen. But she insisted she'd be all right.'

Belle nodded. 'Typical mother's response.'

His smile broadened a little. 'You're right. No matter what they're feeling they still insist they're fine. I should have argued with her.'

Belle stood up. 'I've tried arguing with my father a dozen times and it never does any good. I suppose it's parental privilege.'

'You could be right.'

He was rapidly regaining control of himself, Belle could see. After the initial shock, he was starting to function with his customary efficiency. He looked around the room.

'I don't want to crush Laine's clothes with too many of my possessions, so I'll take just a change of clothes and my shaving gear. Will it be all right if I leave the rest here?'

'Of course. I can send it on or,' she paused, 'you could come back and fetch it as soon as you know your mother's all right.'

His arms went around her briefly, with an instant flaring of warmth. 'Don't worry, I'll be back. You won't have to hold my possessions hostage to get me here.'

He kissed her lightly, his lips capturing hers for only a second, but it was enough to send surges of desire racing along her veins like wildfire. She pulled free.

'There's no time for this now. You have to get packed.'

At the bedroom door, she paused. 'I know you told Laine you didn't want to eat anything, but would it help if I made you some coffee and brought it in here?'

He gave her a grateful glance. 'You're an angel. Coffee sounds terrific right now.'

Thankful that there was something she could do to help, however little, she sped towards the kitchen and filled the kettle with water. While she waited for it to boil, she spooned coffee into two cups. She would have hers with him while he got ready.

That he would soon be gone from the island, she pushed to the back of her mind. His mother was ill and needed him, that was what mattered. There would be plenty of time later for them to indulge the passions which had flared between them in their brief embrace moments ago.

Rex was right about the chemistry which existed between them. It was almost palpable and the slightest contact could ignite it. The touch of a hand, a brief kiss, was enough to set their senses ablaze with need of each other.

Belle hugged herself as she thought about last night. Even though Rex would soon be far away, she was his and the certainty would sustain her until he returned.

The kettle shrilled and she made the coffee, stirring cream into Rex's cup with brisk gestures. He had refused food, but she put a couple of Danish pastries on to a plate, transferring the cups and food to a tray to take back to Rex's room.

She was delayed for a short time when one of
the film crew looked in with a request to borrow
some milk. His work finished here, he was in a
chatty mood and she was thankful when he left at
last. She and Rex had precious little time before he
had to leave and she didn't want to waste any of
it.

Half-way down the corridor, she heard voices
coming from Laine's room. One of them was Rex's
and the angry sound made her pause.

'You'll have to do better than that, Laine.' Rex
sounded angrier than Belle could remember hearing
him.

'Oh, I can do better, much better.' Laine's voice
was an answering purr, so blatantly seductive that
Belle felt ill.

She was shocked at herself for eavesdropping,
but something held her to the spot, listening to the
drama being played out beyond Laine's partly open
door. She was, after all, a part of whatever was
going on.

Even as she rationalised her own behaviour, she
felt a tremor of dismay go down her spine at Laine's
tone.

'Please, Rex, whatever I did was because I care
so much about you.'

Rex's curt response came soon after. 'The only
person you care about is yourself.'

'How can you say that? You know it isn't true.'

Unexpectedly, the door swung open of its own accord to reveal Laine standing on tiptoe with her arms around Rex's neck and her lips pressed to his.

The sight so shocked Belle that she almost dropped the tray. She thrust it on to a nearby table and leaned against the wall for support.

Suddenly she realised she only had Rex's word for it that Laine was his sister. Was it an elaborate lie to get Belle into his bed, where he had made it clear he wanted her from the beginning? If so, she had fallen for it hook, line and sinker.

'My Belle, my wife...' he had said, sounding so sincere. Why, oh why, hadn't she remembered that he was an actor, whose stock-in-trade was deception?

He had deceived her expertly enough. She had totally accepted his story about Laine's past, even to the extent of agreeing to go to bed with him as if they were already married.

What a blind, trusting fool she was!

'Oh, my God—Belle!'

At the sound of Rex's voice, she looked back to find him staring at her in horror. Was he sorry for Belle, or sorry for himself, that his deception had been found out?

Either way, she didn't care any more. She just wanted to get away from the sight of him in Laine's arms. Whatever the explanation, it spelled the end of her hopes and dreams for them.

'Belle, please wait.'

Before he could move, she fled down the corridor and out across the terrace to the beach, wanting to put as much distance between herself and her betrayer as possible.

What could he possibly have to say to her that would make any difference now?

Despite her flying feet he caught up with her at the cove, where she had shown him the best places to dive for coral. When he caught at her arm, she tried to pull free.

'Let me go! Haven't you done enough for one night's work?'

'Belle, what you saw... it isn't what you think!'

She turned to face him, her gaze defiant, hiding the depths of her pain. 'Isn't it? Then what is it, Mister Nice Guy? Are you going to give me some more of that sister-rubbish?'

'No, I'm not,' he said flatly.

So he had decided to tell her the truth at last, for all the difference it would make. 'That's something, I suppose,' she said miserably. 'Well, is Laine Grosvenor your sister or not?'

CHAPTER TEN

TIME seemed to stand still as she waited for his answer, which was an eternity in coming. She was achingly conscious of the suffering in his dark eyes and longed to offer him some words or gestures of comfort. But until she knew where she stood with him, she was unable to reach out.

He looked down, scuffing the sand with his feet, which were clad, she noted distantly, in expensive jogging shoes. For running after women like Laine, she thought with bitter irony.

His words confirmed her worst fears. 'No, Laine isn't my sister.'

Belle didn't wait to hear any more. With an animal cry she was powerless to withhold, she turned away from him and fled across the beach.

He appealed to her to stop, but she was in no mood for his apologies, however sincere. Nothing he could say would alleviate the pain she felt at discovering the extent of his deception.

It must have seemed inspired, saying that Laine was his sister. He knew it would absolve him from all suspicion in Belle's mind. And it had. She had given herself to him willingly, certain that he would marry her as soon as he could protect his mother from Laine's threats.

Now who was to protect Belle? She had given Rex everything of herself and she felt as if she was empty inside.

Although she had changed her clothes, she still wore the high-heeled sandals she had partied in last night, and they caught at every rock and sand drift. But she pressed on, not looking back in case Rex tried to follow her. She needed some time to herself before she faced him again.

Beyond the encroaching mangroves, she knew of a tiny cove outside the colony. There was only a small crescent of beach backed by tropical vegetation. In front lay the coral banks which were exposed in all their magnificence at low tide.

The tide was out now, she saw as she reached the cove. Risking a glance backwards she saw that Rex was nowhere in sight. Maybe he had decided to head back and get ready for the flight to the mainland with Laine.

With Laine. She choked on the thought, but was forced to accept it. After what she had seen in Laine's bedroom, she had no doubt that Laine had achieved her aim of a reconciliation with Rex.

But why pretend she was his sister? As soon as she thought of the question, the answer followed. He had wanted Belle in his bed from the moment he arrived, and the only way to get her there was to make up a sufficiently touching story.

'The bastard!' she said aloud, disturbing a heron which had been fishing in the shallows. It flew off, its wings wide and majestic and she watched it with misty eyes.

'I hope you weren't referring to me,' came a cheerful voice behind her and she jumped, startled.

'Sammy! I didn't hear you approaching.'

If he noticed her wan expression, he said nothing. 'I was meditating behind those rocks,' he explained. 'We're leaving shortly and I wanted to soak up some of this tranquil atmosphere before I rejoin the rat race.'

Although she felt anything but tranquil, she nodded. 'I feel the same way when I have to leave.'

Sammy reached out and touched her cheek with a gentle hand. 'You look pretty miserable for someone who isn't leaving. Anything I can do?'

Fiercely, she shook her head. 'No, but thanks for being concerned.'

'It's a habit I developed from having my own kids. They're grown up now, the son working in films, and the daughter married and living in Western Australia.'

Belle guessed he was talking to give her time to recover her poise. 'Any grandchildren?' she asked, making the most of the diversion.

'Two girls, four and five. They're both as cheeky as their mother ever was.' He folded his arms and regarded her anxiously. 'Feeling better now?'

She nodded.

'Enough to want to talk about it?'

'I don't know...' she said diffidently.

He guided her to his pile of rocks and she sat down beside him, feeling the sun-drenched stone warming her back. 'I gather this has something to do with Rex Marron?'

There was no reason to deny it. 'Yes.'

'When we arrived, I got the feeling that you two were ... well ... close.'

'Close enough,' she conceded. 'But only as friends.'

'But it was turning into something more until we came along, wasn't it?'

She shrugged. 'I don't know. Maybe.'

Sammy let out a sharp breath. 'I guessed as much. And I feel responsible for what's happened.'

Her head came up. 'You? Why?'

'If we hadn't needed your island for location shooting, Laine Grosvenor wouldn't have been able to get her clutches into Rex again. You and he might have made a match of it.'

'I doubt it,' she said soberly. 'I don't think it was ever really over between them.'

'Maybe you're right. All the same, by letting us come here you didn't get much out of the bargain.'

More than he knew! But she wasn't going to toss away what little remained of her pride by telling anyone how she had been duped. 'It's all right, I'll get over it,' she said with forced assurance.

'I hope so. You're too nice a girl to go to waste.'

'Thanks, Sammy. I needed a vote of confidence today.'

He stood up, brushing the sand from his clothes. 'I'd better be going. The crew will be waiting and I told everyone else to be on time, so I should set an example. Will you be all right?'

She attempted a smile. 'Sure, Sammy. Have a good flight back.'

'Won't you come and see us off?'

She shook her head. 'I'll stand here and wave as you take off.'

'That will have to do. I'll let you know how the footage comes out and whether we need you to loop in any of the dialogue in post-production. If not, we'll see you when we screen the rough-cut.'

'I'll be there,' she agreed, not at all sure that she would. Seeing herself on the screen opposite Laine would only bring back painful memories. Maybe she would just immerse herself in her writing and forget all about the film world, which had brought her so much heartache lately.

She waved as Sammy trudged off up the beach. Then she turned her attention to the carpet of coral which was rapidly being exposed by the retreating waves.

Her cove was no more than twenty yards across, hemmed in on both sides by the coral beds. They were drying out in the air now, the beds broken up by small ocean pools and the gleam of stranded seashells.

She focused her attention on the white caps dotting the placid waters beyond the low tide mark.

If only she could float away on the waves, and be free of this aching sense of loss.

Now and again, a wave broke against a giant coralhead, exposed by the low water, and her spirits shattered in sympathy, into hundreds of pinpricks of diamond bright light. She felt as if her heart, too, was breaking into tiny little pieces.

She let her breath out slowly, realising she'd been holding it. Unconsciously, she was listening for the sound of the helicopter.

Sammy had said they were leaving soon. Rex would be aboard, travelling back to the mainland with Laine.

Unless the story of his mother's illness was a lie, too. He had seemed genuinely alarmed when Laine had given him her message this morning, so perhaps that part was true.

It was only the part about Laine threatening his mother's health that he had exaggerated.

She could see why he had done it. She had made it clear that she wasn't interested in a holiday romance, which was what he had first offered. So this was the only way he could entice her into bed.

She stifled a sob. How she wished she could have the night over again. How different things would be then.

But would they? a small voice inside her asked querulously. Would she be any more resistant to his treacherous charms for knowing the truth?

Even now, she could recall the warmth of his hands on her skin, and the mounting excitement

she felt when he had made love to her. Damn him!
He had made her enjoy his lovemaking and she
knew—fool that she was—that she would still fall
prey to him, even knowing there was no future for
them.

'Belle! Belle, where are you?'

She tensed as she heard Rex calling for her, then
looked frantically around the small cove. There was
no hiding place here.

She scrambled to her feet. Now she knew the
awful truth about herself, Rex mustn't find her
here. She would be his no matter what he was, or
what he did. What sort of woman did that make
her?

Before she could frame the answer in her head,
Rex appeared at the entrance to the cove, picking
his way cautiously over the exposed coral beds.

In panic, she ran towards the other arm of the
cove and was faced with more coral. There was
nothing for it but to cross the bed to reach the sanc-
tuary of the mangroves beyond.

'Belle, wait! We have to talk.'

She needed no more impetus to set off across the
coral, but she could only move slowly, hampered
by her shoes which were hopelessly unsuited to reef
walking.

The shtup-shtup of his shoes on the moist sand
told her he was coming this way. She turned to see
how close he was and stumbled on a knife-edge of
coral, falling to her knees.

Instinctively, she put out her hands to break her fall and cried out as the coral bit into her tender palms.

'For God's sake, don't move or you'll only do more damage. I'm coming to get you.'

Caught like a wounded animal in a trap, she could only stay where she was, feeling the coral bite into the fabric of her jeans. Luckily the material was robust, or her legs would have been cut to ribbons. As it was, blood was already oozing from the dozens of small cuts on her feet where the coral had sliced through her sandals. She hardly dared to look at her hands to see what state they were in. They were stinging and she could feel warm blood trickling between her fingers.

By the time Rex reached her, she was shaking with reaction. 'You silly fool,' he said, his voice harsh but gentle. 'Why did you run away from me? Look what you've done to yourself.'

She didn't want to look, either at him or the damage to her hands and feet, so she closed her eyes just in time to stop a tear of frustration squeezing out from under the lids.

She gasped with shock when he swept her up into his arms. 'Put me down, I can walk,' she protested feebly.

'And cut yourself on the coral again?' he said. 'No way, lady. I'm taking you back with me now and you're going to listen to reason whether you like it or not.'

It was useless to squirm, because he held her too tightly, almost crushing the breath out of her. He seemed afraid she would leap from his arms and run away again. 'I heard and saw enough this morning to last me a lifetime,' she said dispiritedly. 'And you needn't hold me so tightly. I'm not going anywhere.'

'Too right you aren't,' he agreed with maddening good humour. He looked down at her tenderly. 'I kind of like you like this, a helpless captive.'

She had been his captive for a long time, she thought miserably, but not in the way he meant. 'You always did like things your own way, didn't you?' she said hotly.

Damn him! She should be fighting like a tigress to make him release her. Instead, she lay meekly in his arms, actually enjoying the warmth of his body through her shirt. As he walked, the motion rubbed her breasts against his chest and she found the sensation acutely disturbing.

'Don't drift off to sleep,' he warned, looking down at her closed eyes, the lashes quivering against her cheeks.

As if she could, when every nerve-ending was alive to his nearness. Despite all she knew of his treachery, she could still react this way. If he tried to make love to her now, she was not at all sure she could refuse him.

But he didn't try to take advantage of her. Instead, he carried her into the villa and set her gently down on the couch, propping her lacerated feet up on a towel.

'Where do you keep your first-aid kit?' he asked in a tone which brooked no argument.

'In my bathroom,' she said, biting her lip at the pain which had started to surge through her feet and hands.

Whether it was the pain of the coral cuts alone, or of being forced into close proximity with Rex, knowing that he didn't love her, she couldn't say.

She forced her eyes shut, making her mind a blank. Don't think, don't resist, just go along, she told herself. He would be gone in a short while and she would have plenty of time for thinking then. And for regrets.

'Hurting, aren't they?' he said, returning with the first-aid kit.

She nodded. 'A bit.'

He opened the box and took out cotton wool and antiseptic. 'I'm afraid this will hurt even more, but those cuts must be cleaned or they could become infected.'

She knew the hazards of the tropics as well as he did, better since she had grown up on this island. 'It's all right, I'm ready,' she said firmly.

The first sharp sting of the antiseptic brought tears to her eyes, even though Rex was as gentle as possible. If anything, the tenderness of his touch made it even harder to bear, because it reminded her of her inner pain which would not go away when the cuts healed.

Then he began treating her hands, wincing as he saw the damage she had done. Her palms were a mass of tiny cuts which stung as he cleaned the grit and sand out of them.

When he looked up at her, his own eyes were moist. 'My poor Belle, what have I done to you?'

'It wasn't your fault,' she said dully.

'If I hadn't followed you, you wouldn't have ventured out on the coral beds in those stupid, flimsy shoes,' he said in a tone of self-deprecation.

She mustered a weak smile. 'You'd think I would know better by now, after all the time I've spent here.'

'Some people just take longer to get a message than others.'

Why did he sound as if there was a deeper meaning to his comment? What lesson did he think she was slow in learning? If it was the one about men's perfidy, she had learned it well and truly, thanks to him.

He held out two white tablets and she looked at him questioningly. 'What are they?'

'Only aspirin, for the pain.'

It would take stronger pain-killers than those to assuage the hurt she felt inside, but she took them and swallowed them with the water he proffered. 'Thank you.'

He took back the glass and set it down, then dropped into the armchair opposite her. 'Now you and I are going to talk.'

'You don't owe me any explanations.'

'Maybe not, but I do owe you the truth.'

She wasn't sure she wanted to hear any more of his 'truths', which were only designed to achieve his own ends. 'Shouldn't you be getting ready to leave with the others?'

He shook his head. 'I've already told them I'm not coming.'

'But your mother?'

'My mother is perfectly all right, as I found out when I telephoned her a short time ago.'

It must be the aspirin making her feel so confused. 'I don't understand.'

'Neither did I, until I called her. It seemed so unlikely that her companion would make such an urgent call and then not insist on speaking to me, so I decided to ring and check the details.'

'I'm glad she's not ill,' Belle said sincerely. 'It must have been a misunderstanding.'

'You could say that.' He broke into a broad smile. 'My mother did say she was looking forward to meeting her new daughter-in-law.'

Belle's heart sank. So this was Rex's way of letting her know that he intended to marry Laine and that he had his mother's blessing. 'She must be very happy for you both,' she said.

'On the other hand, I did tell her the lady hadn't accepted yet.'

Why was he torturing her like this? 'Knowing Laine, the answer should be fairly predictable,' she stated.

'Which it would be, if I was going to ask her,' he said, his eyes tracing patterns down Belle's face.

'If you were going to ask her?' Belle parroted foolishly. 'How else do you propose to somebody?'

Unexpectedly, he dropped to one knee alongside the couch where she was reclining, and clasped her hand, being careful to avoid the coral cuts. "Like this,' he said. 'Belle Fraser, will you marry me?'

She tried to pull her hand away, but he refused to release it and she couldn't wrestle with him without hurting herself. 'Stop this, Rex!' she insisted. 'I know what I saw this morning, and you admitted you made up that story about Laine being your sister so you could get me into bed. Aren't you satisfied?'

He rubbed the back of her hand against his cheek. 'Oh no, not by a long way. It will take many more nights of having you in my bed before I'm satisfied, my love.'

She felt as if she would explode with frustration. 'Then why did you concoct that story about a sister, when you know it wasn't true?'

'Because I believed it was when I told you,' he said soberly. 'When Laine came to my mother, she had all the papers proving her birth and adoption. I had no reason to doubt her identity until a short while ago.'

Belle could hardly breathe for the sense of anticipation building inside her. 'How did you find out the truth?'

'Because I overplayed my hand with that fake message this morning,' trilled a gay voice behind them.

Belle looked up, startled, to find Laine framed in the doorway. She was dressed for travel in a two-piece seersucker suit and straw hat, and carried a cabin bag over her shoulder. 'I came to say goodbye, and heard you two talking about me.'

'You know what they say about eavesdroppers,' Rex growled.

'They may not hear good of themselves, but they do hear the most interesting parts,' Laine countered. 'I'll let Rex tell you the gory details, Belle, but take it from me, it was fun while it lasted.'

Belle regarded her bleakly. 'Fun?'

'Of course. Love is a game, isn't it? Only I lost this time. But not entirely. My career's on its way now, so I got what I came for.' Her eyes swept over Rex with just a trace of regret, before her insouciant expression was back. 'Or most of it, anyway. Ta-ra, you two.'

Then she was gone and Belle sank back against her cushions, feeling breathless with surprise. 'What did she mean by all that?' she asked Rex.

'As she said, she overplayed her hand this morning,' he explained. 'When she suggested I put my things in her case, she thought it would be a cosy arrangement for when we reached the mainland. But she left her passport where I could see it. It didn't match the details she'd given me when she arrived.'

'But it could have been in her adopting family's name,' Belle ventured, more confused than ever.

'True, but it wasn't. Once my suspicions were aroused, I checked her case more thoroughly, a fact I would be ashamed of if she hadn't started this game, as she calls it. I found a card from her mother in England, wishing her well with her sad task.'

'What sad task?'

'To deliver some personal papers from her late room-mate, the real daughter my mother bore all those years ago.'

'Then she wasn't your mother's child at all?'

'No. When I confronted her with what I'd found, she admitted it. By pretending to be my long-lost sister, she'd seen a chance to ingratiate herself with my family and further her career. My real sister died in a car accident. Laine shared a room with her at drama college and knew the facts. She brought the papers supposedly to give to my mother, but decided to use them for her own ends.'

Belle's breath escaped in a whisper of amazement. 'She would have succeeded if she hadn't tried to demand too much too soon.'

'Thank God she did.' Rex raked a hand through his hair. 'Otherwise we might still believe her story.'

'You know, I think she was really in love with you,' Belle observed.

'I doubt whether she loves anyone but herself,' he said scathingly. 'But if she did fall for me, it was all the more ironic because she'd put me off limits by saying she was my sister. I think that's why she was so determined to come between me and any other woman.'

'Will you press some sort of charges against her?' Belle asked, wondering at the same time what they could possibly be.

'I suppose I could, for fraud or attempted extortion or something. But I won't, because the case would only expose my mother to the scandal I was trying to avoid before. She may be improving, but I don't think she's strong enough for that.'

'All the same, it seems wrong that Laine should just get away with everything she's done, almost ruining your reputation for one thing.'

His grin was lop-sided and warm. 'Hardly that. If anything, she's done wonders for my macho image. You should see my fan mail from young women wanting to console me after the break-up.' He paused, thoughtfully. 'At least Laine can't do any more damage, threatening to expose my mother's past. She knows I'll make public her attempted fraud, so we're safe from her for good. Which means I can ask you to marry me, Belle.'

She could hardly speak for the happiness overwhelming her. 'Yes, Rex,' she managed at last. 'I'd be honoured to be your wife. Except——' she bit her lip.

'Except what?' he prompted.

'You know what they say about show-business marriages. So few of them seem to work out.'

'I have the answer for that,' he said after a pause. 'One of us will have to give up show business.'

'Then it had better be me, since I'm half-way there already with my writing plans.'

He kissed the top of her head lightly, sending shivers of pleasure coursing through her. 'Of course, Sapphire and Rafe, I'd almost forgotten. Tell me, do they live happily ever after in your book, too?'

'Of course,' she said demurely, thinking of the glorious ending she had already drafted for her characters. Then she frowned. 'I thought you said you'd read *Sapphire Nights*.'

'Knowing you saw me as Rafe to your Sapphire, I was afraid to read the last pages in case things didn't turn out the way I hoped for them.'

'And have they?' she asked.

'They have now you've said yes,' he responded gruffly. 'I wonder how Rafe sealed his promise to Sapphire.'

'Like this.' She tilted her head to his, her lips moist and inviting. When he claimed her mouth in a totally possessive, demanding kiss, she knew he understood her answer.

'So this is what a happy ending feels like,' he murmured against her mouth.

She didn't argue but, as she gloried in the feel of his strong arms around her, she knew it was only a beginning.

ATTRACTIVE, SPACE SAVING BOOK RACK

Display your most prized novels on this handsome and sturdy book rack. The hand-rubbed walnut finish will blend into your library decor with quiet elegance, providing a practical organizer for your favorite hard-or soft-covered books.

Only $9.95

Approximately 16" x 8" when assembled

Assembles in seconds!

To order, rush your name, address and zip code, along with a check or money order for $10.70* ($9.95 plus 75¢ postage and handling) payable to *Harlequin Reader Service*:

Harlequin Reader Service
Book Rack Offer
901 Fuhrmann Blvd.
P.O. Box 1396
Buffalo, NY 14269-1396

Offer not available in Canada.

*New York and Iowa residents add appropriate sales tax.

BKR-1A

HARLEQUIN SIGNATURE EDITION

JUST ONE NIGHT

Hawk Sinclair—Texas millionaire and owner of the exclusive
Sinclair hotels, determined to protect his son's inheritance.
Leonie Spencer—desperate to protect her sister's happiness.

They were together for just one night.
The night their daughter was conceived.

Blackmail, kidnapping and attempted murder add suspense
to passion in this exciting bestseller.

The success story of Carole Mortimer continues with *Just
One Night*, a captivating romance from the author of the
bestselling novels, *Gypsy* and *Merlyn's Magic*.

★

**Available in March
wherever paperbacks are sold.**

WTCH-1

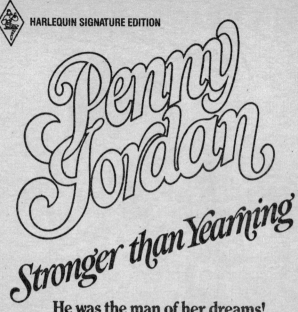

HARLEQUIN SIGNATURE EDITION

Penny Jordan

Stronger than Yearning

He was the man of her dreams!

The same dark hair, the same mocking eyes; it was as if the Regency rake of the portrait, the seducer of Jenna's dream, had come to life. Jenna, believing the last of the Deverils dead, was determined to buy the great old Yorkshire Hall—to claim it for her daughter, Lucy, and put to rest some of the painful memories of Lucy's birth. She had no way of knowing that a direct descendant of the black sheep Deveril even existed—or that James Allingham and his own powerful yearnings would disrupt her plan entirely.

Penny Jordan's first Harlequin Signature Edition *Love's Choices* was an outstanding success. Penny Jordan has written more than 40 best-selling titles—more than 4 million copies sold.

Now, be sure to buy her latest bestseller, *Stronger Than Yearning*. Available wherever paperbacks are sold—in June.

STRONG-1R

Give in to Temptation! Harlequin Temptation

The story of a woman who knows her own mind, her own heart ... and of the man who touches her, body and soul.

Intimate, sexy stories of today's woman—her troubles, her triumphs, her tears, her laughter.

And her ultimate commitment to love.

Four new titles each month—get 'em while they're hot. Available wherever paperbacks are sold.   Temp-1